MW01254440

MIND SET OF A
GOOD PERSON

MIND SET OF A GOOD PERSON

LEO AGWU

MIND SET OF A GOOD PERSON

Copyright © 2020 Leo Agwu.

All rights reserved. No part of this book may be used or reproduced by any means, graphic, electronic, or mechanical, including photocopying, recording, taping or by any information storage retrieval system without the written permission of the author except in the case of brief quotations embodied in critical articles and reviews.

iUniverse books may be ordered through booksellers or by contacting:

iUniverse
1663 Liberty Drive
Bloomington, IN 47403
www.iuniverse.com
1-800-Authors (1-800-288-4677)

Because of the dynamic nature of the Internet, any web addresses or links contained in this book may have changed since publication and may no longer be valid. The views expressed in this work are solely those of the author and do not necessarily reflect the views of the publisher, and the publisher hereby disclaims any responsibility for them.

Any people depicted in stock imagery provided by Getty Images are models, and such images are being used for illustrative purposes only.
Certain stock imagery © Getty Images.

ISBN: 978-1-6632-0409-7 (sc)
ISBN: 978-1-6632-0410-3 (e)

Library of Congress Control Number: 2020911897

Print information available on the last page.

iUniverse rev. date: 06/27/2020

DEDICATION

TO: THE SOUL OF CHUKWUMA AGWU, EMMY IJEOMA OMELEBELE, OLIVIA ONYEJINDU CHIDEBE

And the souls of the children all over the world who died, the very day born to this world.

LEO	Father
John /Fredrick	Son
Michael Mole	(Irish boy)
Tony Hugo	(Best friend of Michael)
	Mix compilation
Betty Hugo	(Toni's Mom.)
Brenda Bee	(Toni's classmate)
Two police officers	(Who first arrested Tony)
Ann	(Friend to Betty)
Lawyer Cohen Bob	(Toni's Lawyer)
Dr. Anthony Three(?)	
May	Secretary to Cohen
Maxine	the wife of Dr. Anthony
Vincent Mark	(The shot dead teenager)
Bay Bee	(Brenda's Mom)
Kate	(Lulu's Mom)
Vera Elu	(Judge of the case)
Prosecutor James	(Prosecutor of the case)
Bishop Victor Bobe	(Toni's Bishop)
Carthrine	(Church member)
Debora	(Church member)
John	(prison death row)

CHAPTER 1

J/F: Dad I am confused about how some people are so good and some are so bad. Why is it this way?

LEO: We have to start from the human foundation which started

1. From the day a child was born till the child turns three years,

2. A child, from three years till 10 years.

3. 10 years to adolescent

4. Starting relationship which may lead to partnership

5. Form a partner

6. What is foundation to happy relationship and what lead to bad relationship?

As a child was born, I mean from the day the child was born, the child is innocent, with clean mind. If you bring new born babies, Kim from China, Ngozi from Nigeria, Lisa from America, Veo from North Korea, Elizabeth from Britain, Mary from Colombia, Maliki from Sudan, Anthony from Barbados. Let's say, new born babies from different Countries, all the Continents, put them in one room where they would be with one another without their parents being there. They will cry when hungry, wet, feel heat, or when they need comfort. As you do their needs, they will stop crying, because they do not have time to play politics. They will see each another as the same because of no prejudice envy in them, hatred of any kind, no competition. Feed them when needed, change them when needed and coddle them when needed, there will be no complain because their needs are met. No lion kill two animals at a time, eating one and save the other for tomorrow or python killing two animals for feeding at a time. As long as their needs are met, they will no more be bothered. Keep ten to twenty babies from different continents, meet their needs as mentioned above, let them be cared for by people from different continents, the children will not know the different if one is White, Black, Chinese, Indian or Nigerian, they will play together as one as long as you do not bring their mom there, because they will, due to natural law, noticed the touch of their mom when presence. This is the angelical stage. I call this stage angelical because at this stage, they are sinless, trust and love every one that shows them a little love and they don't play politics, they do not have sense of siding Peter or Paul, Mary or Uche, White, Black, Chinese or Pilipino. This is the group I love most. Until they start identifying this and that person, now getting attached to people, (around 2 years)

The stage of inquisitive, very energetic, but still don't know what is dangerous, still very attached to people they see constantly like mothers, dad, kind of fearful of strangers, do not like to be separated from people they are used to, stage trying to say some words at all time, playing with anything, playing with others but may not be able to share things like toys because they think everything belongs to them. This is when memory starts to improve, knowing some food flavors she/he did not like, stage when they move very fast without considering the dangers ahead but with lot of emotions.

People need to protect them because they do not know the difference of good and bad but the most clean minded stage. This stage of trying to listen more, trying to do as told, like let us go to the car, table, the room, or outside, but very challenging, stage when they easily say no or why, cry to get their ways, very temperamental. At this stage people should be very careful what they say/do when with the child because it will come out of their mouth without thinking of who hears it, they still do not know much difference only copycatting.

You are now with a person who may turn out good or bad due to how you started or set up the foundation, remember that if you want a plant to bend to the left or right, you do not wait till the plant formed trunk before you start forcing it to the direction prefers but should start bending it or guiding it to your preferred direction which will be easier than before the old tiny plant formed trunk,the stage when you either brake your back or cut down the plant because it will not go your way, the same to children.

So at this stage please start doing good corrections because the life dance just started of which whatever you teach the child will go a long way which might extent to future generations. As above mentioned it will go a long way but they are still innocent, most things they do is what they got from adults around them.

CHAPTER 2

Michael Mole from island started kinder garden with Tony Hugo from America, both very attached as friends till the sixth grade, no different is noticed between this two friends only that Tony is dark while Michael, Lighter as his from Island, both do everything together, they feel bad every Friday because they will not see till Monday when they come back to school. At 12th grade Michael invited Tony to his birthday for Saturday and as Tony got home, he informed his mom.

Tony: Mom, you know Michael is doing his 16th birthday on Saturday, he invited me as his best friend to be there on Saturday. Even told me that we all are going to sleep over till Sunday, the next day.

Mom: But you do not go for sleep over, I do not think it is a good idea even though you are best of friend, anything can happen over there, then you will be blamed for what you don't know, Tony I am older than you, what an elderly can see while sitting down, a young child can not see it even when sitting on the top of the mountain, you are all I have.

Tony: Mom, some time you begin to think as if you are 90 years, don't worry mom nothing will happen on Saturday, I will sleep over because if I don't, all my classmates will make fool of me as they will call me all kind of names like chicken or baby.

Mom: Okay if you think so but what the elder noticed while sitting, a child can be on the mountain without seeing or noticed it.

On Saturday Toni's mom bought a birthday present for Michael and Tony in the afternoon was dropped by his mom to Michael's house for the party. (Tony is filled with happiness) all their classmate including the girls came prepared to sleep over as part of the birthday party. The party started and

4

every one enjoyed themselves, after the party, everyone went to where to sleep, in the morning Brenda Bee was very sad, crying that someone stole her Gucci bag with all her belongings.

Brenda Bee: Michael, someone stole my Gucci bag where all my belongings are, please ask everyone if they know about it or mistakenly took it.

Michael Mole: Please guys, Brenda is looking for her Gucci bag, if anyone of you have it please bring it out.

After searching everywhere unsuccessfully finding it, every one left to their home. On Monday while everyone was in the class, Toni's attention was called by the principal to come to the office and tony left to the office but as he got there, two police office were in the office.

Principal: Tony, where is Brenda's Gucci bag? There is information that you stole the bag.

Tony: What are you talking about?

Principal: You see the two officers, they are here to arrest you but I told them to let me talk with you first.

Tony: I don't know anything about the bag, I don't have her bag. I don't have her bag.

Principal: Officers, he told me he doesn't know anything about the bag.

Officer: Then he is under arrest.

Tony was hand cuffed and taken to the police station.

Officer: we want you to tell us where you kept the bag.

Tony: I don't know anything about the bag, I don't have the bag. Please can I call my mom?

(He was given a phone to call. Phone range and Toni's mom picked the phone.

Tony: Crying and saying mom, I was arrested by two police officers.

Mom: Why? For what? Where is the station?

Tony: St James station. Please come as soon as possible. (So she hurried up).

Betty Hug Toni's mom rushed to the police station only to be informed, she should wait for the next one hour till the interrogation, she waited while crying, she was not informed what really took place. After one hour, she was told to go to room 6 where she can speak to Tony for twenty minutes.

Betty: (Seeing the son standing to speak with her behind the glass, started crying but picked the phone and asked) Tony what happened to the point of police picking you from school. Please tell me exactly what happened that made police to arrest you from school, (as he, unstoppably crying) please stop crying and tell me what took place at school.

Tony: Mom, it was not at school, they told me that I stole Brenda's Gucci bag. Which I did not, I don't even know how Gucci bag look like,even stealing it, mom believe me, I did not steal no bag.

Betty: But why did the police picked only you? If I may ask, how many boys where there, how many black and white boys where there?

Tony: Mom, I was the only black boy there but it had make no difference since we started growing up, I don't see any of the boys different, we all do things together without seeing any difference. but what happened now made me looking at things different because this Brenda don't like blacks, I know it because last year she was putting me down because of being black, it was Michael that stopped her from her foolishness by asking her if she is as smart as me? Tried to let her know that the color of the skin made no difference.

Betty: Did you tell police what you told me now?

Tony: No mom, they didn't even let me say anything but asked me to sign a blank paper but I said "No".

Betty: Drop the phone, I want to go and get a lawyer to start defending you out of this racist behavior, hold your head high. We will be here tomorrow. Try to sleep, you will be out of this place as soon as possible because you don't belong here, no matter what any police do or tell you, do not change from the fact as you know it.

Tony: Mom, don't worry, it will be okay at last because I did not do anything as accused.

As Betty left the detention, she went first to the church to pray for God's guidance in this problem. (God please I beg you for Toni's protection in this case, I beg you for the vindication of my son Tony, let the fact be known no matter who is at fault. Please guide me as I now start looking for defense lawyer to take care of this case). After praying and crying in the church, she left to Ann's house, her friend. As Ann Opened the door, Betty started crying.

Ann: What is wrong? Is Tony okay? Why are you crying?

Betty: Ann, Tony went to little Michael's house a few days ago, it happened that someone stole one of the girls Gucci bag, the girl got home and told her parents that Tony stole her bag, reported it to the police who went to the school on Monday and arrested Tony saying that he was the person who stole the Gucci bag. I was called by Tony from the detention where I went to see and talked to him. The poor boy was crying, saying that he never did as stated and I believed him, Tony don't steal, what is he going to do with Gucci bag? This is a girl who never liked him since lower grade in the school calling him half half.

Ann: What is half half?

Betty: As mixed race, she even according to Tony told him as a mixed race, that Tony will end up mentally retarded also as mixed race, that Toni's life expectancy will not pass 40 years which I disputed it to Tony.

Ann: We have this Jewish good, lawyer Cohen but he is only very expensive.

Let me call him at least to know if he is in town because he always travels, Betty, don't worry, it is well this is why the wise people say never say never because tomorrow is pregnant, no one knows what she is going to have, boy or girl. She dialed the number.

Ann: Hello Cohen, how are you doing? Are you in your office because we are coming to see you.

Cohen Bob: Good afternoon, yes I am and expecting you

Ann: Betty, let's go to his office now, crying is never going to save the situation, the more you cry, the more you get discourage because you think the world has now fallen on you and Tony. Who even know where Anthony is now? I know he will not want to be involved in this case, the boy he denied from birth saying he never made love with you let alone being responsible for the pregnancy, a lot of people including me was even having double mind then because we were young, but me or any one now who see Tony and him even though he is lighter complexions, will not say that he is not the father, Tony so resemble him, the way he walk, look, even smile, the only thing they don't have in common is stealing and going to jail, remember he used to be in trouble then. Do you remember William, he is rich now

Betty: William Gonys, he used to go to jail, who will see him now, believe that he used go to jail for one reason or the other but mostly fighting with Anthony. Thank God Tony did not inherit fighting from Anthony, also stealing which have never happened before this case. He told me he did not and I believe him, Tony hated the two bad characters of his dad, mostly stealing but the intelligent of Tony came from his dad, even though I am intelligent I know he got mathematics from him because I hated mathematics all my life and mathematics was Anthony's favorite subjects.

Do you know lately Tony is being saying mommy I want to be a doctor like my so called dad, since we got the news that he is a doctor. I know he eventually will be a doctor like his dad. Anthony was some how good even though he never accepted Tony due to stupidity, shame that he impregnate a black girl, but look at it, the wife now from what I heard cannot have baby, coming clean and accept Tony as his son could have been good. Do you remember saghie? He told me Anthony will soon try to make peace with me and came for Tony.

(Now Ann and Betty got to the lawyer's office).

Ann: Good afternoon – (secretary to Mr. Cohen) We are here to see Cohen.

Secretary: Good afternoon, get seated, does he know you are coming to see him?

Ann: Yes

Secretary: Okay I'll let him know when he finished the conference meeting.

Betty: Thanks. (They got seated waiting for the secretary to go and let Cohen know of their presence).

Secretary: Excuse me sir, there are two ladies one of them called Ann come to see you, can they come to your office now?

Cohen: Let them in side.

Secretary: You can go to see him.

Betty: Thanks.

Betty/Ann: (together) good afternoon Cohen,

Cohen: Good afternoon too, how are you doing Ann? How is your family? I hope all is well?

Ann: No, unfortunately I am here with my friend since 3rd grade,she is Betty Hugo the son is in a very bad situation.

Cohen: Ms. Betty what is going on.

Betty: My son Tony was invited to get together in his friend's house, some of their school classmates included, after the party on Saturday, on Monday my son Tony was arrested by two police officers saying that he stole Gucci bag that belongs to one of his classmate by the name Brenda, this girl who could not stand my son because he is a mixed race, she voiced it out in the school, she do not speak to my son, according to my son, they did not talk to each other at the party, my son told me he never see her with any bag as she came into the party, shot he did not do what he is accused of doing. Now languishing in police detention, police forcing him to accept taking the bag but my son told them no because he did not steal the bag. Please can you defend my son? Or if not,can you find him a good lawyer to defend him?

Ann: He is the one to defend Tony, please Cohen, when soonest are you going to see him, talk with him then tell us what to do, I don't want him there by tomorrow, when are you going there? I know other lawyers but this is your case, go there, talk with him then tell us what to do and cost to defend him. Thank you. (She smile)

Cohen: I will be there in the next two hours, I will give you the estimate cost by tomorrow. I might put motion to bail him as soon as I finished speaking with him this evening. You say he is a teenager but what age?

Ann: 16yrs.

Cohen: Pressed the bell button for the secretary to come, (as she walked inn) pleased take all the information needed from Betty.

May: Betty come with me (she now go to the secretary's office with her, where all the information needed were taken. It was while taken the information from Betty the secretary found out that Tony was mix race, child of Dr Anthony three who is Mr. Cohen's client and a good friend. As she finished taking the information, went to Cohen and informed him what she just found out.

May: Do you know that Dr. Anthony is the father of this Tony boy we are talking about? (Cohen called Betty back to his office and this was how it went).

Cohen: Ms. Betty can you tell me about Dr. Anthony who happened to be my very good friend and never told me about Tony.

Betty: Dr. Anthony was my first hidden childhood boyfriend, made me lose my virgin at 16 but denied ever done anything like having sex with me let alone getting me pregnant, I was shamed by everyone for not knowing the real father of my baby to be but I knew I never had sex with anyone but him 4 times before I found out I was even three months pregnant. I had the child then gave the name as Tony because Anthony is the father. When you see him you will see for yourself then pass your judgment.

Cohen: Let us go now to the detention this is getting more interesting. (Three of them, Cohen, Betty and Ann left to the detention).

CHAPTER 3

As they got to detention, filled the necessary forms by Cohen as Toni's lawyer and the two women were allowed to wait in a room for Tony. As Tony walked to the room brought by the warder, Cohen saw Tony, he look at Betty. This is Dr. Anthony's child and I will talk with him as I get home this evening, no way, something good is going to come out of these to both you and Dr. Anthony, you see how things happen for a reason, Cohen introduced himself to Tony as his lawyer and more to be.

Cohen: Tony how are you doing? How are they treating you here? Do not hide anything from me, I am your lawyer to help you.

Tony: I am sad because of been accused for what I did not do. They are not treating me badly except police officers in charge of this case trying to make me accept what I never did but I will never admit what I never did even though a gun is pointed on my head.

Cohen: Tell me what happened.

Tony: I was invited to Michael's birthday party in his house on Saturday, as I got to his house, most of my classmates were there, we all enjoyed ourselves, l slept over though I never do so but Michael is my childhood friend. The next day (Sunday) I left back to my house, I did not come with bag, not even sleeping bag and I went back as I came (nothing) on Monday I was in the class when the principal sent for me to come to his office.

When I got to his office, two police officers were there, I was introduced to them by the principal as a very good boy. He then asked me if I took Brenda's Gucci bag the day we went to the birthday party? But I said "no" I came empty handed, left empty handed, you can ask Michael who walked me half way to my house before he went back, he will tell you I did not carry even back pack, No, No, No, I did not take it. After talking to the principal, two police officers said "you have to come with us to our office first." I was handcuffed, taken to their station, interrogated for 2 hours, telling me to accept that I took the bag out of mistake but all the time, I told them that I did not steal the bag and nothing in this world will make me accept what I never did.

Cohen: Betty let us go but we will be back in the evening.

Betty: me and you?

Cohen: No, me and Dr. Anthony.

Betty: Why? And what made you think he will now want to see his son that he all along denied as his son?

Cohen: Just leave me do what I have to do, how can Dr. Anthony see this boy, duplicate of him still say he is not the father of this boy.

Betty: Okay but how much is going to be your Charge?

Cohen: Dr. Anthony will pay not you, so don't think of the fee, his father will pay whatever I want him to pay, it is no more your cup of tea, be open minded everything will walk out fine, something good will come out of this unfortunate arrest, bye to two of you.

CHAPTER 4

lawyer Cohen went back into his office, place call to Dr. Anthony

Dr. Anthony: Hello Cohen, What is going on for you calling by this time?

Cohen: A lot, we have to see today as soon as possible, where can I meet you? This is something to discus one on one, face to face, not cell phone discussion please I have to see you asp.

Dr. Anthony: What is going on? Why do you want me as soon as possible.

Cohen: Dr. Anthony, why did you always say you don't have children?

Dr. Anthony: Why all these? Do you know what I don't know about me?

Cohen: I just discovered what you know all along. Is Tony not you child? Have you ever see him in person? If you ever seen him, you would have known that he is your duplicate, 100% you. Only younger.

Dr.: When and where did you see this Tony you are talking about?

Cohen: He is in detention and I will like both of us to go as I am going for his bail today.

Dr.: What took him to the detention?

Cohen: Please I had what happened between you and Betty (he was wrongly accused) but whatever that took place between both of you should not be extended to the child, you in person must do something about it. Let us go there for you to see for yourself. (He convinced Dr. Anthony to go visit detention which he did, both went inside, requested to see Tony as his lawyer, now waited until Tony was lead out to see them.

Dr. Anthony: Crying and said "Tony are you ok"?

Tony: Yes sir. (This is the first time seeing Dr. Anthony) (Dr. Anthony crying and listing to lawyer Cohen and Tony till he can no longer take it, then got involved by asking the lawyer the cost to handle the case).

Dr. Anthony: What will be the cost of this case? How do you bail him.?

Cohen: You are more than qualify to bail him.

Now Cohen called the guard to go with Tony and say to Tony, you may go home this evening so put your fingers cross. (Tony left with the guard).

Dr. Anthony: please what do I do now? You know all that took place between Betty and I Was just childish,I got myself so deep in lying hole that even till now I don't even know how to turn all the bad things to Betty and this boy around, please you are now the Dj, I will dance any music you play but first of all let's work on his bail now.

Lawyer Cohen worked out how to bail him and he should be bailed and signed by the mom or the bailer who should be around him all the time till the next court day. (Now Cohen called Betty to come immediately to the detention to sign as the bail had been made. As she got there to her greatest surprise, Dr. Anthony was there, crying as he asked her how she is doing?

Dr. Anthony: I hope you and my son will have the mind to forgive me for all I put you two through, but I promise you two, things will change positively, you don't deserve what you went through, even the boy,though it was childish that made me do all the nonsense I did then but I am now a complete changed man.

Betty: How is your family? I hope all is well? if you will accept him, will you ever show him his siblings?

Dr. Anthony: He don't have any siblings, I am married and as of now we are in process of divorce.

Betty: Why? But you said you are a change man now? First of all have you seen Tony? Did you introduce yourself to him? How did he feel seeing his father for the first time?

Dr. Anthony: She is the one filling for divorce saying that I can not produce a baby. I did not introduce myself to him but he was just looking at me. I bailed him, you are now to sign for his custody, to be around him till the next court day. Now lawyer Cohen, the guard and Tony came out and called Betty to come and sign but she read the condition after giving them her driving license as I.D, she read it again and asked,is his father not going to sign too? And Dr. Anthony said, "I signed already". Tony knew something is going on, the way Betty, lawyer Cohen and Dr. Anthony were behaving. Now Betty did the interdiction.

Betty: Tony do you remember the story I told you about your dad? here is Dr. Anthony.

Dr. Anthony went to tony to hug him and three of them started crying.

Lawyer Cohen: Nothing happened for nothing, may be this is the way the movie was written, I know we all have a lot to talk about but Tony should go home first as he is very tired.

Dr. Anthony: (He hugged Tony and as he hugged Betty, wisped: you will one day be my wife.

As they were going home, Tony asked the mom how the man he never met since he was born now come to know he got arrested, now started playing such role of bailing and trying to act as family member?

Tony: Mom you told me this man abandoned both of us when you got pregnant, now here he is, who told him what happened to me to the point of him bailing me from detention?

Betty: It is a long story but we will talk about it as we get home.

As Betty and Tony (the son) drove off going home while Dr. Anthony could not bear the situation, turned around only to follow Betty and Tony behind, he followed them till they got to their place, got out of her car surprisingly noticed Dr. Anthony also getting out of his car too.

Betty: laughing, shaking her head and say to Dr. Anthony: what are you doing here? I thought you left to your place, I didn't know you are following us.

Dr. Anthony: I could not bear talking to you two and just go home, please can I come with you two into your house? Please say yes I want to talk to you two.

Betty: Why not, come but the house is a little messy, I have being going crazy since this incidence took place, I thought this is the end of my life because if anything happen to this boy (Now crying) I will kill myself but not knowing that the pregnant mother nature have something strange for us, my grand mom usually say that tomorrow come with unexpected package, anything is possible in this life.

CHAPTER 5

(As they got inside Dr. Anthony kneeling down).

Dr. Anthony: Betty and Tony, no matter how I say it, how much cry and tears in my eyes, it will never fix all that I put two of you through since Toni's conception till now, please Betty I did so much bad to you, no matter what I say now, it will be very difficult to change all the bad situation and shame I put you and your family through.

Why it hurts more is that, your mom past, not seeing this situation, your exoneration for what you was say then, how will one see Tony and me without saying that he is my son, I was a big fool then, I believe nature know how to fix situation, it made me not to be able to have another child after all Maxine and I did, going from one gynecologist to another, all came to the same result.

Till I saw Tony, life was no more meaning to me hearing words from her mouth like "you are not a man enough to get a woman pregnant", even telling me to give her permission to have sex with men out there to prove me wrong, that the problem of us not having children came from me not her, to the point now of us divorcing each other thank God, I did not context it, you ask lawyer Cohen, he is my lawyer too, he was so mad at me for never acknowledging that I had a son, today is my happiest day, I will pay any price you two want me to pay.

My dear Tony, I was such a fool to denied having anything to do with your mother let alone getting her pregnant, I was a child then, what do I know, but what happened is going to teach so many people a great lesion because nobody knows tomorrow. Please Tony, I am your father, deserted you and your mother all these time, please forgive me for all the bad things I did to you and your mom (Betty) like I said "I will pay any price you two want me to pay but for two of you to forgive me and accept me back into your life, I will never separate from both of you and as the divorce take place, I will propose your mom to please accept to be my wife and if she do accept, we will have a very big wedding and live together for the rest of my life, I could not go back to my house, this was why I turned around only to follow you two, please Betty and my son Tony please forgive me, nothing like this will ever take place again. Tony what is your favorite food out there?

Tony: Pizza.

Dr. Anthony: Betty can you order pizza for three of us at least, we got to start from somewhere. (Betty ordered the pizza while Tony went to take his shower and Dr. Anthony walked to Betty held her and both of them had a very hot kiss and Dr. Anthony saying to Betty I will sleep here tonight, don't say no, let me sleep here tonight. The pizza came, Dr. Anthony gave Betty $100 bill to go and pay for the pizza and she came back with $60 change but Dr. Anthony told her to keep it).

They all ate, Tony was just looking, confused, don't even know what to say but kind of happy for being out of detention and seeing his father for the first time, at last went to his room to sleep while Dr. Anthony and Betty in Betty's room, had a very long talk but at last slept together and history repeated again, were both very happy through out the morning. Dr. Anthony called lawyer Cohen to let him know of the latest development. (As Tony went to his room).

Dr. Anthony: Betty, can we have some private talks in the room?

Betty: Okay, come with me to my room.

Dr. Anthony: With the name of the spirits of love, please forgive me for all the childish, stupid, bad and wicked treatment I exhibited towards you when you got pregnant of Tony, it was childish confused as a child could be, stupid for not being reasoning, bad and wicked as I never cared how you and the baby felt then till now ten hours ago, let us not dwell on the past, to be able to see the future, let's discus how to make Tony feel good at this moment and let's this night be our new beginning, I know all will be well if you are willing, convinced Tony that I made so much mistakes in my past life, this is one of them and believe me, I paid a lot of prices for being childish, stupid, bad and wicked then but now a changed person, please let's make each other better, historic, and positively talk of town, a case book and story good to read forever.

Betty: come inside the bed all is well as long as we will not allow pressure of the world destroy us three again.

At 10am Betty woke up, took her shower, prepared the bathroom for Dr. Anthony to go and take his shower which he did but as he was taking his shower, Betty made breakfast for three of them, set the table and as he came out of the bathroom Tony went to him, hugged him and Betty joined them as they all went to the dinning table and ate their breakfast very happy, all smiling.

CHAPTER 6

They started their breakfast, while the television on, the flash news came saying that a teenager by the name Vincent mark 17 years got shot dead, suspect at large. At 12 o'clock, Brenda said to her mom.

Brenda Bee: mom I know who must have killed Vincent, it is no body but Tony Hugo.

Keisha Bee: Are you sure?

Brenda: yes, he came out yesterday and did it at night because Vincent knew that Tony was the person who stole my Gucci bag and agreed to testify against Tony.

Keisha: Stay at home, I am coming back very soon.

Now Keisha went to her friend (Kate,Lulu's mom) who also friend of Brenda, of which was in the Michael's birth day party, she now talked to Kate on the information she got from Brenda, who went to the police station to inform the police of Tony been the killer of Vincent. As Brenda's mom left, Brenda phoned Michael as he was alone at his house, started talking to Michael to say Tony phoned him last night saying that he is going to kill Vincent Mark for saying he is going to testify against him as the person who stole my Gucci bag.

Brenda Bee: Michael, you know you've being asking me out, promising to do anything for me just to agree to date you, are you still interested? I want you to say that you told me that Tony phoned you yesterday and told you he is going to kill Vincent as he want to testify that Tony stole my Gucci bag

Michael: Yes, but I did not even know that Tony came out of the custody yesterday, let alone him coming to see me or call me. How can I say so?

Brenda: Michael I will be in your house soon.

Michael: Okay.

Brenda: (Now in Michael's house, show her nakedness to Michael) Michael can you see what I have for you for the rest of our life? (She pulled her skirt down and show her nakedness to Michael, asked him don't you think all these, touching her breast and her lower part, belong to you) came close to me, (as Michael got close, she grabbed him and gave him a very hot kiss). Are you willing to testify against Tony)?

Michael: Okay, I will.

(Brenda now grabbed Michael's hands and placed them on her both breast, kissed him then left back to her house.) Before you know it, three police officers, her mom and Kate came to speak to Brenda in her house

Police officer: What is your name?

Brenda: Brenda Bee.

Police officer: How did you get such information that Tony Huge killed Vincent Mask?

Brenda: Michael Mole, best Toni's friend told me that

Tony called him last night, told him that he is going to kill Vincent Mask for saying that he is going to testify against him, because Vincent know that Tony stole my Gucci bag. Tony is very wicked, you should all arrest the bustard, he has a gun and always say how much he feel killing police.

Police officer: Thank you, we will call on you one of these days.

As the officers left, they went to Michael's house, interrogated him and he confirmed the story as Brenda told them, now the three officers left to Toni's house, now knocked at the door.

Dr. Anthony: There is some one knocking let me go and see who is at the door.

Betty: Anthony, you are the man of the house, you are right, go and see who is at the door.

Dr. Anthony (As he got to the door, police officers were standing with their guns pulled): officers what is going on?

Police officers: Hands up, face the wall, freeze, we are here to arrest Tony for killing Vincent Mark last night.

Dr. Anthony: How?, he was bailed last night let me show you the bailed paper. Why is the world so wicked (now want to take the bailed paper out of his pocket, one of the officers pulled his gun and fired on Dr. Anthony and he went down as he was shouting why, why).

Betty: (Crying, asking) Why did you kill him,(kneeling and with Tony around Dr. Anthony Crying).

Police officer: Let one officer call for ambulance please. Young man, are you Tony?

Tony: Yes, why did you kill my father? We only met yesterday?

Police officer: You are under arrest, now you hands on you back. (Tony was handcuffed), You are to be taking to the station for the murder of Vincent last night (at the same time the ambulance taking his dead father to the hospital while Betty stoned confused but calling God, asking him, why,where are you? Are you sure you exist? But before taken Tony to the station, their house was searched, founded no gun, the officers asked for Toni's gun but Tony and his mom told them he has no gun.

Betty: Dialed the phone and called lawyer Cohen.

Cohen: Hello, how is Tony? Is he doing okay?

Betty: No, we are not doing okay, your friend Dr. Anthony was shot dead by police about 2 hours ago.

Cohen: What are you saying? I don't understand what you are saying. Can you repeat what you said?

Betty: (Crying) police officers shot and killed your friend, Dr Anthony about 2 hours ago.

Cohen: I am on the way to you place, stop crying.(As Cohen managed to drive to Betty's place, officer standing at the scene,introduced himself to the officer.

Cohen: Betty what do you say took place to the point of police shooting and killing Dr. Anthony? Where is Tony?

Betty: Three hours ago we had a knock at the door, as we Dr. Anthony, Tony, and I were having our breakfast, Dr. Anthony went to the door, I had him asking "what is the problem"? Then other voices say your hands on the wall, before I know what was going on, I heard gunshot, now Dr. Anthony saying why, why, Tony, and I went out at the same time only to meet Dr. Anthony gasping and dying while the officers confused but looking, doing nothing but at last my son Tony was asked to identify himself which he did, then one of the officers pulled his gun saying, "young man your hands on your back" Tony crying but with no word, put his hands on his back, he was hand cuffed, then the officer said "you are under arrest for killing Vincent last night. Where is the murder weapon? Both of us told them that Tony came out of custody last night, he did not kill anyone.

Cohen: Betty let's go to the station right away.

They left to the station, as they got to the station, introduced themselves to the officers.

Lawyer Cohen: Officers, can I see who is in charge of this mess.

Officer Victor: I am in charge of the case.

Cohen: Can I see Tony? Just for fee minutes.

Officers Victor: Okay but you got to fill this form before I can do as requested.

Cohen filled the form, show his identification and Betty's identification too. The officer left, came back with Tony who had been tortured during the interrogation, Tony looked at the mom as both were crying.

Tony: Mom how can I kill Vincent last night when we were all at home? And why should I kill him? I don't even know where he live but most of all I was at home with you and daddy all night.

Betty: First of all I know they are accusing you wrongly, you are not the killer, even though pregnant monkey said that she can not deny any crime accused of her child carried at her back but will always deny for the child in her womb, but in this case I will bet my life saying that you are not the killer, where do the officers thought you will get gun used to kill Vincent? They searched everywhere in the house without any trace of gun.

Lawyer Cohen: Tony,I finished reading their report saying that you committed the crime at about 10pm last night. Where were you at 10pm last night?

Tony: With my parents, I went to my room at 11pm and did not step out of the house. It was not me at all, why should I kill Vicent? Any way God knows that I did not go out last night, let alone killing Vincent.

Lawyer Cohen: (Went to the officer). Please I will like to cut and preserve some of Toni's hair today.

Officer: As you requested, I will order it done, when next you come I will give it to you sir. I want to take him to the custody now.

(Tony was taken back to the custody and the mom and the lawyer left.)

Betty: Cohen, why did you requested for his hair sample? What do you want to do with it?

Cohen: A lot, some will be taken for gun powder residue which is always left on the hair of the shooter of any gun.

Betty: What do I know, only think I know is that Tony did not kill any one, people always say never say never but in this case if there is God, he knows my son Tony did not do such a crime, he was with us at home through out last night till the time picked up this morning after the police murdered his father for no reason saying they thought Dr. Anthony was bringing out a gun.

Cohen: Let's go but come to my office tomorrow after 2 o'clock because I will not be back from court till 1:30pm. Go home, don't worry, I believe all is well.

CHAPTER 7

The next day Betty and her friend Ann went to see the lawyer as the news of Tony killing Vincent and Dr. Anthony been shot dead by police, spread all over the town. Police went and interviewed Michael who now told the police that it was Tony his friend that told him he was going to kill Vincent for knowing that he was the person who stole Brenda's Gucci bag and he called me last night at about 1am telling me he did it. Now policed warned him not to discuss anything he told them with anyone but to keep it secret, as police left Michael, he call Brenda.

Michael: Hello, Hello Brenda, police just left our place after a long interview about Tony and Vincent.

Brenda: Why don't you came over, my mom is not home, come let's play.

Michael: I am worried what will eventually happen to Tony, you know he is still my best friend.

Brenda: Not any more, I am your best friend, may even eventually be the mother of your children as your wife, are you coming or do you want me to come over your place so that you can show me a strong man you are? Is your mom at home?

Michael: Okay you can come, my mom is not at home, she will be back around 7pm.

Brenda: I will be there very soon. (Brenda went there after 20 minutes, knocked at Michael's door.)

Brenda: (knocked) Michael opened the door.

Michael: Come inside, how are you doing? I can't believe Vincent is dead, I was told Tony is in custody and the father shot dead, what a tragedy.

Brenda: Let us go in your room and do something as the beginning of our love life.

Michael: Okay, come with me to my room. Though it is not clean, but when next you come, you will see it well clean.

They went inside, made quick love and after the love making Brenda stole Michael's cell phone as Michael went to take a shower and as Michael came back, she rushed back home but before she left, she reminded Michael never to change his statement he gave the police because it could lead him to prison if he changed his statement given to the police. As she left, Michael went to sleep, woke up started looking for his phone, was not man enough to go and ask Brenda for his cell phone though Brenda threw the cell phone into the small river knowing well police may check his phone to find out if Tony called Michael to tell him he was going to kill Vincent. The fear of discovery made her plotted stealing and throwing the phone into the river.

All these went round the town, as the news got to Brenda's mom, she now know of Dr. Anthony's death though she never knew of Dr. Anthony been living in town since their teenage time when Anthony one time love making lead to the pregnancy of Brenda which she never discussed with anyone as her mom died shortly as she found out she got pregnant, also Anthony left the town to cover up the shame of getting the black class mate (Betty) pregnant which lead to birth of Tony.

Brenda's mom now, realized Tony and Brenda, two weeks birth apart are half brother and sister, but unknowingly Brenda hated Tony since 4th grade for no reason. She cried about it but could not tell anyone not even Brenda. The next day Betty went to Lawyer Cohen (as planed).

Betty: Good afternoon Cohen, how are you doing?

Cohen: Afternoon Betty, I don't know how am feeling, trying to think why so many thing took place asking myself if there is God for real, or is more than 60% of the world been manipulated by making them believe there is God? Because sometimes I do get confused of what people go through in life. I wish there is a way everyone could use (telescope) to look and check how their life in the world he/she is coming is going to be, I think the population would have been as much because after seeing what the person will go through in life, he/she will say forget it, I am going to stay in the spiritual world than coming to the land of living and go through all the nonsense ahead of my life.

Betty: Both of us have the same but different level of thought because I use to say to myself, I wish people should have something to check how the future of their marriage will be before they get married.

Cohen: No one could have gotten married, I think that could have been better, after all animals don't get married but still have young ones. I will not lie to you, above question bothers me a lot and the more I thought of it the less answer I get. Betty, but how was your last two night but tragic reunion with Dr. Anthony?

Betty: Everything was so perfect, we even made love and slept together not knowing that tragedy was on the way, two of them (DR. Anthony and Tony) were so happy and quickly bonded as if they knew each other for a long time, though people always say that blood is thicker than water.

When we went to bed, Dr. Anthony was so remorseful for what he put me and his son Tony through in life, even say nature punished him not to have any other child even when he got married, begging me to give him a second chance to fix the damages he made. But did I know that the same person will be killed few hours from then? Will I know my son who slept in the next room will be charged for the murder he never committed? Cohen, it had been said that monkey told the other monkeys in their colony, that she love and trust her baby, but she will not trust him as much as the one in the womb not out in the world yet, she will always trust her more that the one out in the world but I bet you with my life, my son Tony did not kill

Vincent,that night he went to his room and slept off at 12:30am, I checked to make sure he was sleeping at 2am before Dr. Anthony and I started making love, I even checked him at 3am as I went to the wash room, just to be sure he was asleep while we were doing it, he was sleeping. So when did he committed the murder? Few days ago he was in police custody till the day you got him out, can you put it together? Because I can't.

Cohen: Me too, I can't but believe you, I believe it to be false accusation but you know this is a journey of 100 miles which starts with a foot step, it is not over till it is over, I will see to bottom of this, you are not going to pay me anything because I know I will be paid in future when I will sue the police for wrong accusation and the city will pay it.

CHAPTER 8

They went to Toni's first court hearing for bail but was refused bail now set for the hearing on April 10th 1999. The burial of Dr. Anthony brought almost all their past classmates as news spread like dry desert burning fire, even the mom of Brenda, Keisha who went and hugged Betty.

Keisha: Please forgive me for the childish comments made on you then, please understand it was due to jealousy, wait and hear what we both have in common with Dr. Anthony. This is unfortunate life tragedy, it is a big cross everyone have to carry but all I can ask is where is God? Where is he when all these were taking place? How can he allow all these to take place because we were told in book of Genesis that God know the past, present and future, so he knew and let all these to happen.

Some believers will say God just want to teach us live lessons, what is the lesson here? I don't get it, but let me take your phone number because we have a lot to discourse. How is Tony? Please tell him I say prayers for him (now crying and walked away knowing fully well that Tony and Brenda are half siblings without anyone knowing it but only her).

After the funeral, everyone went their ways, lawyer Cohen and Betty left, seeing each other and preparing for April court hearing. Cohen tried many times in police station for the disclosure of the case file but with no answer only hearing from the police that there is very credible witness to prove Tony to be the killer of Vincent and no one else.

Now on April 10th 1999 in the court as everyone in town came, Judge Vera Elu got to her seat while everyone standing, sat on her seat.

Judge Vera Elu: Good morning everyone, I greeted you good morning because I have to do so but there is nothing good about this morning when we want to start such a pathetic case of two young life been wasted, one is dead while the accused killer's life will never be the same. So what is good about the morning? Both families will never be the same.

The only order I'm give you all in my court is to try to be respectful to one another, I will not tolerate any indecent behavior from any party in this court Because I want to see the bottom of this case which kept me sleepless unlike cases handled before in my 35 years as a judge. I don't know about you all but to me, the more I try to stitch the turned cloth the more it tears but I had made up my mind, Promised myself that as long as the sky will not torch the ground, as long as snake will not give birth to goat or dog give birth to snake, I will see to the end of this case. Please let us not be carried away, let us all collectively put our heads together, see that the head of the snake is chopped off from the body of the snake, because unit the head of snake is chopped off, it will still be scary, so let's begin.

Prosecutor James: Before starting, I want them to bring the monster into the court by the name Tony Hugo.

Judge: Refrain from the word monster and I will not correct you any more, no one's name is monster, if you want the accused by the name Tony to be brought into the court room, say so, please don't make the case journey too long by getting carried away by emotion. start now.

Prosecutor: I am sorry your honor, (cleared his throat). Before starting, I will like the police to bring the accused into the court (Tony was brought into the court, looked at the crowed in the court also the mom,then started crying). On January 4 1999, a young prospect boy of this community was at 11:45pm shot and killed, no suspect found but as the news spread, the police was given the information of the killer, who was arrested the next day and in the process of arresting the accused, his father was mistakenly shot dead as police thought his father was pulling out a gun.

We got full information from a good friend of the accused person boasting of killing Vicent Mark for witnessing him stealing a Gucci bag that belong to Brenda, the very day they went to home birth day party. The person killed is Vincent Mark, a 17 years respectful boy who lost his life for knowing the truth and wanted to tell it all, but to stop him from letting the cat out of the bag,the accused by name Tony Hugo decided to stop him from testifying against him, told his friend who will appear to testify on the matter" I will kill Vincent for trying to testify against me" and he carried it out by killing him with gun, in the process of arresting him by the police, the father was shot and killed.

The name of the diseased person in this case is Vincent Mark 17 years, you all know him but for the recording, made me giving his name in full, he was shot at the parents doorstep at 11:45. On January 4th 1999, he died on the way to the hospital. The name of the accused who is in the accused chair now, who is known by most of you is Tony Hugo, 17 years but to me as the prosecutor of this case, I will like him charged as adult for such a heartless, barbaric killing over simple Gucci bag. The judge refused him bail because of flight risk.

Tony Hugo, can you stand and identify yourself.

Tony Hugo: (Standing by him is the lawyer Mr. Cohen). My name is Tony Hugo 17 years.

Prosecutor: Repeat after me as you have the bible in your left hand and raise your right hand "I Tony Hugo, solemnly swear that all I will say in this court will be the truth, the whole truth so help me / God (repeated by Tony).

Prosecutor: On January 4th 1999, you after talking to a good friend of you by the name Michael Mole 17 years, that you are going to get reed of Vicent Mark for saying that he will testify against you for stealing Brenda's Gucci bag, you went to Vincent's family's house, ambushed him and shot him as he returned home trying to open the door.

Judge: Tony, did you hear the statement by the prosecutor?

Tony: Yes your honor.

Judge: Guilty or not guilty?

Tony: Absolutely not guilty your honor.

Prosecutor: You will be proven guilty very soon.

Lawyer Cohen: (Toni's lawyer) Your worship how can you prove that Tony who was with parents after been bailed from custody the very day, did not go anywhere the very evening of the event, committed this crime?

Prosecutor: Called for Michael Mole to appear as witness.

Judge: Race your right hand and repeat after me (I Michael Mole solemnly swear that evident I will give in this court shall be the whole truth, nothing but the truth, so help me God).

Prosecutor: Michael, do you know who is sitting in the accused seat?

Michael: Yes sir.

Prosecutor: What is his name? How long do you know him? And who is he to you?

Michael: He is Tony Hugo, I know him for 11 years and my best friend. (Brenda was so fixed her eyes on Michael)

Prosecutor: Who is the deceased person?

Michael: Vicent Mark.

Prosecutor: How long do you know him?

Michael: 11 years.

Prosecutor: Who is he to you?

Michael: Classmate.

Prosecutor: If I should ask you who is closer to you and who do you care for the most out of these two?

Lawyer Cohen: Your honor, Objection.

The Judge: Answer.

Michael: Tony Hugo.

Prosecutor: Did Tony Hugo ever say to you that he will get reed of Vicent Mark for saying that he is going to testify that Tony Hugo stole Brenda's Gucci bag and he went and killed Vincent Mark?

Cohen: Objection your honor.

Judge: Refrain Prosecutor.

Prosecutor: What did Tony Hugo say to you when he knew Vicent Mark planed to testify against him stealing Brenda Bee's Gucci bag?

Cohen: Objection, due to the speculation.

Judge: Answer it.

Michael: He told me that he is going to get reed of Vincent as he is going to testify against him for the stealing of Brenda's Gucci bag.

Cohen: Michael, what is your relationship with Brenda, Vincent and Tony? Where is your cell phone.?

Prosecutor: Your honor, the question is too ambiguous, should be refrain from such question.

Cohen: Okay, what is your relationship whit Brenda? What happened to your cell phone?

Michael: A friend and till today, I don't know, still looking for it.

Cohen: What is your relationship with Vicent Mark?

Michael: A classmate.

Cohen: Were you not the person who walked Tony Hugo home from your house the day after the party? And do Tony Hugo have a cell phone?

Michael: Of course yes, he don't have a cell phone and I don't know who's phone he used.

Cohen: What was he carrying as he was walking home from your house?

Prosecutor: Objection, this is not about stealing of the bag but about killing of Vicent Mark.

Judge: Answer.

Michael: I don't know.

Cohen: What did you tell your principal when he questioned you about the Gucci bag?

Prosecutor: Objection, the lawyer is trying to confuse my client.

Judge: Answer.

Michael: I did not remember.

Cohen: If I have to remind you, did you not tell the principal that you walked Tony half way home and he was not carrying anything not even backpack.

Michael: Yes.

Cohen: For recording, say what you told the principal.

Prosecutor: He is barging the witness so can you tell the defense lawyer to stop barging the witness.

Judge: Michael yes meaning what? Tell the court and that will be the last answer.

Michael: I told the principal that I don't (Brenda focused her eyes on him) remember sir (the prosecutor corrected him, your honor not sir).

Judge: The court adjourned till tomorrow for my Verdict.

Court **clerk**: arise (everyone did so and the accused was taken away, the judge left and everyone left) Betty, lawyer Cohen left.

Cohen: Betty, From my observation, Michael whom you told me is Toni's friend nailed him in all the angles, I believe the judge believed him and he is going to find him guilty, all I will be begging the judge to do is leniency, to consider him as minor not adult as the stupid prosecutor is asking for.

Betty started throwing up, the lawyer thought it was due to heartbreak but as she started passing out, he took her to the nearest hospital where they told her that she is pregnant which was mix blessing to her but she confide with Cohen that the very night Dr. Anthony slept in their house, they made love few hours before he was shot and killed. Lawyer Cohen dropped her back to her house, told her to be ready by 8am tomorrow.

The next day as court was more filled than yesterday, the judge sitting on his chair, clears her throat.

Judge: We have to follow proper court procedures for the future reference. The two lawyer will be given chance as requested, by the defense lawyer. So the prosecutor should do the closing first.

Prosecutor: You honor, it is unfortunate that the city is losing two young boys, one by the name Tony Hugo who viciously murdered Vicent Mark for trying to be a good citizen, planning to testify that he saw what took place, not minding his friendship with Tony Hugo,not like most of the young boys who will pretend not knowing of the stealing of Gucci bag by Tony Hugo, not knowing that it will cost him his life.

We are still scratching our heads, asking ourselves what do Tony Hugo wanted to do with female's Gucci bag? The closest answer to me is that the water you see flowing in the river did not start from the spot, it started flowing from far away, what I meant was, the death journey of Vicent Mark must have started from Tony Hugo's stealing Brenda's Gucci bag. My prayer is that the worse is over, looking at the life lost.

There is someone not talked much about in this sad story, Dr. Anthony Three, what a sad event. I wonder how Tony Hugo will be feeling knowing fully well that all these started from stealing of the Gucci bag that belong to Brenda Bee,the killing of innocent boy Vincent, the mistake shooting of Dr. Anthony Three and the life time the defendant is going to serve though still have a chance of living. If left to me, I will make it death penalty, people should stop crying, we all should only pray for such sad event never to be fall our beautiful, peaceful city again, what a waste, what a waste. your honor I rest my case before I get emotional.

Lawyer Cohen: Let's not prejudge innocent, misfortune boy Tony Hugo who fell from frying pan to fire, let us know that the wise mom said, "when you use big knife dismantling the head of chimpanzee, please be touching yours too because there is no much different from yours as human", We should all think of all these set up, it can happen to any of us one day. Brenda Bee, Michael Mole, the police, people of our city, this is not going to be the end of Toni's life story but l know he is going somewhere. Jonah in the bible was instructed by God to go and preach to people of Nineveh but boarded a ship to Tarshish until caught in a storm, fell into the water, swallowed by a big fish, carried to Nineveh and vomited over there, did not die, it was a miracle because he could have died, started preaching the gospel of God.

The same gospel God had asked him to go and preach in Nineveh. Tony,don't cry, only your God who know the past, present and future, who knew everything in this your unfortunate life journey, only God know that something good will come out of all these, I sympathize for the life of innocent child Vincent Mark, my bleeding heart go to his family.

The innocent Doctor, Dr. Anthony Three, what of poor innocent Tony Hugo, who thought he finally found his father, not knowing he will only enjoy what so many of us took for granted like it was said. "The boy who often have sex with the family's house girls, will not know that there is scarcity of girls until the family's house maid leave or quit the job". Poor Tony Hugo as I mentioned, only enjoyed having knowing his biological dad for just one day before the rootless police officer took him away from Tony, barbarically murdered him by shooting.

What a tragedy. What about his woman (pointing to Betty) who few days ago thought to be finally exonerated, you all knew the story 18 years ago, when she mention that Anthony Three who later became Dr. Anthony Three got her pregnant, no one believed her story, the shame of how can people believe he had sex with a black classmate by the name Betty Hugo, due to racism, but few day ago, she thought the truth finally came, now exonerated, not knowing what was coming after her.

Betty take heart I know you are a person with deep faith in God, so many people by now could have started doubting if there is God? The God you believed and have faith on, will surely see you through, you remembered what happen yesterday, another chapter in your life, it had been said that the God that show the wivabird the ripped Palm fruit, will protect the wivabird from getting blind as she want to pluck the ripped palm fruit. I know that God will see you through, it is not the end of the story if you believe in God you serve, again what a sad story.

Your honor, these were all set up, believe you me, if it is not a set up, where is the Gucci bag which innocent Tony Hugo told the world he got nothing to do with the bag. Think of it, "The man that stole the king's trumpet, where is he going to blow it, because he will be caught since the king's trumpet is unique. I asked for the witness phone, now the so called Toni's childhood friend could not find it, what a joke and pathetic set up, everyone should hear me clearly, the day of the truth will come when all in this court will say to one another, did you remember the speech of lawyer Cohen in the closing argument in the court? Your honor, Toni's life is in your hand, you should use your long serving experience to know that these are all but set up even though you want to do otherwise, be merciful. Look at Betty Hugo, give Tony Hugo and the mom another chance in life. I still after all the home works I did, beg you to dismiss this case and find Tony Hugo not guilty. Your honor I rest my case.

The judge call for court adjournment till next day for his final verdict.

Court clerk: All stand as the judge walked out of the court,Tony Hugo with hand cuff lead out of court and everyone left to be back tomorrow.

CHAPTER 9

The next day, the Judge sitting, cleared his throat then opened.

Judge: I, many times mentioned that this is a tragedy that fell on this community, please let's not get carried away, I will pass my judgment based on the information we got from the police, prosecutor, defense lawyer and the body movement in the court here, everyone is not going to like my judgment but I still have to do what to do based on the power given to me in this court. After reviewing everything which started from the birth day of Michael, Michael implication of Tony in the killing of Vicent which was quite unfortunate, Michael cell phone which is nowhere to be found, signs giving people during testifying which I noticed but pretended not noticed also the circumstances in death of Dr. Anthony Three who was with the son for only one day, what a tragedy, I ask Tony, not his lawyer, to stand and from your heart address this court with no interruption, anyone who try to interrupt him while addressing the court will be charged with contempt of my court which will not be good, I really mean it. Tony, stand and address the court from your heart.

Tony: Good morning your honor, good morning everyone in this court. I am very sorry to say things that I have no choice but to say not withstanding the consequences. I am saying this to the hearing of the whole world, I never stole the Gucci bag that I was accused of stealing by Brenda Bee, she know in her heart that she wrongly accused me but I have forgiven her. I never mentioned to Tony that I will get reed of Vicent Mark for saying that he was going to testify against me, I am sorry he is dead and there is no way he could say his own side of the story because I never knew of such story, again Michael Mole who happened to be my childhood friend, testified against me wrongly, only him know that he lied.

He told you all that I phoned him telling him that I am planning to kill Vi cent Mark, where is the phone I called him? According to him, still looking for it, maybe he will say that I came from the custody to steal his phone too, Michael you know in your heart that you lied, why? Only you know, but I pray,like Apostle Paul who was approached by God in acts of the Apostles in the bible, I really being praying to God to make you see the light of God, accept him in your heart and you will be a different person. For your wrongly accusation of me, I had forgiven you only pray for God to forgive you too.

The parents of Vicent Mark, please you should take heart, I prayed for your endurance but one thing I am telling you is that I never killed your son Vicent. My mom, take heart, you thought me how to be Godly and be strong, I am begging you now to do the same, No matter the outcome of the judgment, keep your shoulders high, don't feel disappointed because I did not steal Brenda Bee's Gucci bag, I did not tell Michael Mole all this nonsense he told you the court that I, Tony Hugo told him and as he sit in the court looking at me, he know that he lied then, lied today and if he don't confess today, he will still lying against me tomorrow. The reason for doing this, I don't know but had forgiven him, leave him with his God and wish him the best.

Finally to the family of Vicent Mark, my heart go to you for your lose but I never killed your son Vicent. Before I forget, thank you lawyer Cohen for all you did for my family in this case and most of all, helping me to meet my father, God bless you and he alone will reword you. Thank you your honor but all I said then and now is that no matter the outcome of your judgment, I never committed the crime of stealing the Gucci bag, never mentioned to Michael what he said I did and I did not kill Vicent. Thank you.

Judge: Once upon a time, Ubulu town got divisional conflict of which half of the town went into war with the other half, one side called Alumu lead by Edo and the other side Ogbe lead by Ogbue. Edo never go to war only govern by giving instructions but Ogbue been a warrior always in the war front, was terrorizing the Alumus but the worst part of the Ogbue's history was, Obgue happened to be the nephew of Edo, whom Edo used to love as the son of his sister who got married from Alumu to Ogbe.

All Edo hear from the war front is the terror of Ogbue which became a concern, so the chiefs called an emergency meeting on what to do about Ogbue. Dasi was appointed as a warrior in Alumu side, the chiefs went inside the inner chamber, came with resolution to fine a way to kill Obgue. They came out,informed Edo their plan then told leader Edo to announce their resolution and instruction. Now it was a big thought for Edo to give instruction to kill his nephew Ogbue, instead, Edo instructed war lord Dasi who is to lead the full battle to the Ogbe. Edo said "warlord Dasi, we went inside, met, decided that with enough man power given to you to end the war, there is no way you can stop this war when Ogbue is still the leader and warlord of the Ogbe.

I Edo, now give you the power and instruction to lead all this fighters to conquer the Ogbes so that this battle will come to an end and for us to have full confidence of the conquer of the Obges and the battle come to end, do not kill Ogbue but do not allow Ogbue to escape from the battle, I give you my blessing with power given to me. Now Dasi asked Edo, you don't want us to kill Ogbue and you don't want him to escape from the war, how? But Edo told him to use his discretion.

Now back to the judgment. After going through the reports and witness, what most troubles me was the last statement of late Dr. Anthony Three "how can Tony whom I bailed at 3pm from police custody, straight to the mom's house, stayed together in the house till this morning, how can he kill someone outside when he did not go out of the house". This was his argument when he was shot.

The Most damaging witness was the statement of Toni's friend Michael Mole. After going through the above mentioned on January 10th 1999, Tony Hugo I found you guilty for the murder of Vicent Mark but no death penalty, instead, you will go to jail for 20 years with chance of parole after 7 years if well behaved. I will instruct the warden to study and know what you will learn while in prison. Good luck. Do you have anything to say?

Tony: Yes your honor. Brenda and Michael I forgive you two from the bottom of my heart, best luck. Mom go, hold your head high, I will be back one day, to you all in the court, I love you all. (With his hand at the back, handcuffed and lead away by the police). Everyone left the court room but Michael could not leave until was asked to leave,it was due to guilt in his heart for what he just did to his best friend.

CHAPTER 10

The first night of Tony Hugo in his twenty years sentence was very reviling in the sense that in the dream, he found himself as a child sitting on the right lap of his father Dr. Anthony while Brenda also as a child sitting on the left lap of Dr. Anthony, both as Dr. Anthony's children, Dr. Anthony advising them to always love each other more than anyone else. Then he woke up, immediately prayed for Brenda, thanked God, praised him saying it could been worse and it was while doing the devolution he decided going to pastoral school while in the prison which is going to be paid for by the government, saying I must turn the negative into positive so that I will be proud of myself, see this as good omen instead of bad.

On Monday Tony Hugo was introduced to a female case manager who will be in charge of his life for the next twenty years. The case manager was so surprise to meet Tony so happily prepared for the 20 years prison journey unlike the cases she managed before. She introduced herself as Esso.

Esso: Good morning Tony Hugo. I am your case manager for the next 20 years. How was your last night?

Tony: Ms. Esso, please can we first of all kneel down and pray, praise God for this great opportunity in life (as Esso knelt down Tony extended his hands holding Esso's hands) Oh my heavenly father, I thank you for all you have being doing in our life, thanks for all the blessing and opportunities you have being giving us but this opportunity given to me now is a jackpot. I promise you lord with you power behind me, I will climb the mountain, get to the summit and light up the fire which will shine to be seen all over the world, I pray that you will give sister Esso your grace energy to do the climbing of the mountain with me. People call her case manager, but I will for the rest of my life call her my sister, work with her to see our meeting as blessing (at this time Esso started crying gently, all she just saying are amen and thank you God. She never believed in God.) May you receive your two new servants, my father and Vicent, please lord my God put them in good positions in your heaven, please guide my mom, make her see me now as having my B.A. not as doomed. let her see this as a blessing, also I pray that brother Michael and sister Brenda will receive your blessing, turned around and praise you, accept you as their all and all. I pray that all my city will found your blessing as way to come closer but not to separate from one another, not to see each other as white or black but as human because, hatred starts from differentiation, seeing this as black and the other as white. May the Judge found peace in the judgment, not see herself as destroying a young life but in few years see me as blessing, make me a good citizen for all to be proud of me but not to see me as evil to the city and mankind. All these I pray and ask for your anointed blessing, Amen.

Esso: Thanks you God (she still crying) thank you pastor Tony. In my 10 years of case manager, I have never witnessed such or experienced what just took place, how long have you been a pastor? What is a B.A.

Tony: I am not a pastor but it was in the night God blessing came to me and in my mind decided to go for pastoral school while in the prison. At the beginning of Christ ministry, Christ say to peter, instead of going to leave as a fisherman, come with me as a fisher of men for the work of almighty God, with no waste of time peter joined Christ which made him his first Apostle .B .A means, begin again.

Esso: I am your first caught fish and ready to go places and work with you, I can't even tell you how I am feeling now. One question I want to ask you by the end of your first month, after you must have pasted five prison stages of emotion. Denial, angry, acceptance of where they are, planned how to survive the situation and starting the journey of prison. It is in my page 40, for formality because I have the answer now but will still ask. what training will you like to take while in prison?

Tony: pastoral school.

Esso: You have it, I will register you next Monday.

Tony: Sister Esso, please when coming next, can you reach my mom, tell her to buy me bible. You will see her number in my file.

Esso: I will call to see her but you mom is not going to get such glory of been the person that bought you your first bible, I am going to seize such opportunity, I will buy you your first bible, are you kidding me? Never, it is an opportunity which I will not let pass me. Can I hug you, brother Tony?

Tony: Of course. (They hugged) and Tony went inside the prison.

As Tony got to the dining room for lunch with about ninety prisoners in the dining room, he got up and said "brother please let everyone stand, let us pray first, no matter your believe", (like magic, everyone got up).

Tony: Oh God my savior, we your children praise, worship and thank you for this opportunity of being together, I pray that this lunch will never be forgotten by any of your servant given the opportunity to be here in your presence, I pray that everyone here will see coming to this facility, no matter how or what brought him here, as blessing and assignment, Jonah in the bible was asked by you to go and preach to people of Nineveh but in his mind he decided to do something else at the river, then fall into the mouth of big fish, which took him all the way to Nineveh, did not die, and the fish vomited him at shore of the river in Nineveh,he woke up with no question, started the preaching work assigned him to do. So my brothers, from now on, see each other as brothers here going to a journey, no matter what the number of years, months, weeks or days left, use it as opportunity and it may never come your way again.

Thank you God,let sit and eat. The prisoners started saying to one another, maybe he is Christ, just pretending to be a prisoner. They ate lunch with so much and different kind of happiness, spread the good news to the warden who now eager to see Tony for prayer.

One day as they finished praying before eating which is now a practice in the prison, one of the death row inmate Prisoner, close to his dining table begged him if he can speak to him when they finished eating and Tony say yes. They finished, the old man who had being waiting with anger for the day to be executed, told Tony that he had a very terrible dream last night, found himself in the darkness being guarded by lions,the gate all around him locked but suddenly one of the big lion came to him, say to him "sit on my back" which I did, then the giant lion took me to the gate used it's teeth to brake the key at gate, carried me to the day light, dropped me there and went back, then I woke up. I know I might be called to be executed anytime now. I have been in death row for ten years.

Tony: Praise God, your freedom is in front of you.

John: (The death row inmate) I pray, because when they call me and execute me, the pain and torture will end.

Tony: I don't mean to be executed, I meant your final freedom, end of you prison, forgiven of your prison. Thank God, may your plan be done to your servant John. They were on this when a warden came for John saying "you have a visitor, come with me" and john did.

Jonny (Johns case manager): John, there is a development in your case, you've being saying that you was not the killer of the police, eleven years ago but there was so much evidence, testimony against you before the Judge and that was why you was found guilty, sentenced to death, you was to be executed next week but another police officer hearing the news of the plan to execute you, went to his boss and confessed to be the killer of the other officer with the private gun given to you to handled the day he arrested you, you remembered telling the Judge you wasn't the shooter and the Judge told you how did your finger prints all over the gun took place? You told him the police told you to handle the gun with no bullet in it, but no one believed you. The way things are going, your may found your freedom very soon. I just came to give you the good news, bye for now. (They go opposite way)

John ran to Toni's room, getting there, Tony was praying for another very violent inmate asking for God's blessing and peace. But John could not wait for them to finish their prayer, cried and said "you are Christ, stop deceiving us, you are Christ, not inmate, like you told me 40 minutes ago, I am going to be free very soon but not to be executed as planned, the police who first arrested me on the very day, gave me a gun to handle, the gun where my finger print was all over it. It was the killing gun which the officer told the court was found in me, which lead to my found guilty, it belong to the officer and he was the killer.

Tony: Who told you all these?

John: You, indirectly, no, no, the visitor who just visited me is my case manager, she came and broke the news saying that the officer confessed for the crime, now under arrest but you knew already.

Tony: (Praised God, praying and thank God. Now the news spread in the prison.

CHAPTER 11

John the death row inmate was freed after few days. As the news spread in the prison, everyone now coming for prayer from Tony, even the warden now coming for prayer from Tony. He was registered for pastoral school, doing very well to the point that a hall in the prison got opened for Sunday mass service for the prisoners. Almost all the prisoners now converted to Christianity, the warden and outside people from prison came for service in the prison Church only to hear preaching and prayers from miracle man Tony, even his mom comes to the prison church every Sunday. In one of the moms visit, Tony noticed the mom kind of adding weight so he asked the mom.

Tony: Mom, what is going on? You are kind of putting on weight.

Betty: My dear Tony, you are having a brother in couple of months.

They went inside for the day service.

Tony: Before we start service today we have to all get up and clap for God for all he had done for our life without us paying back, even some time get mad at him due to disappointment in life, any time we have a little hiccough in life, we forget all he did already. Like the 99 year old man with twelve children, 30 grandchildren, 60 great grandchildren, 12 great great grandchildren, all alive in different works of life. There is no field you cannot find in this family, the old man and his 89 years old wife in good health, not been in the hospital for the past 30 years but woke up a day to the wife's 90th birth day only to found the wife dead at sleep. The old man was so mad at God, called God all kinds of names asking God why are you this wicked to this family? even regretted believing in God all these years. Can you believe it happens to so many people who do not have the faithful light and blessing, my brothers and sisters, we have to always be grateful for all God does for us, even while in graveyard burying one of our own, we still have to give him praise, in prison we have to worship and praise him, no matter how you found yourself in the prison, knowing full well that you never committed the crime though people still found the ways to collaborate but to found you the innocent person guilty. People who know you, after hearing and seeing the evidences may even start imagining you to be living a double life. It will be so real to the point, that you the innocently accused and found guilty may start hallucinating, confused and start asking yourself, did I do this? You should always know yourself more than anyone, know what you did or not, except under influence of one thing like drug or alcohol. If gold should rust, what in the same condition will happen to iron? If you now don't believe yourself, what about others? They had seen and heard so many evidence, seemed so real that even your love one as the Judge may have no choice but to found you guilty but it was collaboration, well planned but not the truth. At the same time some of us in prison are in prison due to their own making, some are here for one bad crimes or the other, some crimes committed by some of us here are so scaring come to think of it, you might start getting scared of yourself, will not like to be in the same room with the person who committed such a vicious crime, but too bad, you can never run away from your shadow but there is one but one prescription, the only prescription is to repent, accept God in your live, pray for forgiveness, if opportune to see the person victimized or the family if dead, ask them for forgiveness. Forgiven or not, you will feel better,also when people ask for your forgiveness, if you don't forgive the person due to anger, do you know what you are doing to yourself? Self victimization because instead of forgiving, be free minded, you will be more heart broken which could physically, mentally and psychologically affect your health and may lead to you death just because you refused to forgive. My brothers and sisters even when found yourself in any of the above mention, get up sing, clap,let's praise and thank our God because he is so good and sweeter than the honey, he gave the people who gives us, like people we depend on, example, our parents, friends, Billionaires one way or the other depended on him. Mom do you remember the very day I called you from my first visit to police custody? What about the very morning my father was shot by the police and killed, I still remembered your look, crying as police was putting handcuffs on me while my dead father whom I knew and enjoyed for one day lay dead in front of us, do you visualize your face when I was found guilty for a crime I never committed? How do you think I could have been here in this journey without all those travelling tickets? And it is not over yet, only him my God above knows where the journey is going to end but just believe that a journey of 100 miles begin in one step. Thank you my God, thank you God (all say halleluiah) dancing and singing, the service for the day ended as everyone hugging each other, hopping for next Sunday.

As the service ended with much happiness wishing for two service or bigger space for service as the hall kind of tight for the number of people attending the Sunday service. Now people departing from the service, as usual practice, Tony knelt down praying for everyone home going safety but this very day not only praying for people's home going safety, now praying for God miracle for bigger space for service.

As he finished, open his eyes, got up from kneeling only to see the prison chief waiting for him with his wife who got breast cancer.

Tony: Good afternoon sir, good after afternoon madam.

Prison commissioner: Please can you pray for my wife, we found out last two days that she has breast cancer, confused though will be seeing group of doctors on Tuesday to know what to do next.

(Tony asked her to kneel down, which the husband and wife did).

Tony: Thank you my God, this is one way to prove that you are you and no one else even the doctor know the prescription but you, I know with you, there will be now surgery done to this you servant, she will go to see the doctors on Tuesday only to be told to go home, it was a wrong diagnosis, we could not see any cancer cell. I know you my father will do it. I was here praying for a bigger space not knowing that greater request from your servants are coming which I know you will do it, but Oliver still ask for more, I still ask you my heavenly father for more space where Lisa your servant in a bigger crowd will proclaim the great testimony, telling everyone that she was told by the doctors due to result of the test done on her, that she has breast cancer but my God say no to the result, your own test say no breast cancer, I know this will happen next Sunday by your power. My sister get up, you will see, stop crying, you will see that there is no doctor more powerful than God, just ask and you will find, go home in peace.

Prison commissioner: Thank you. We have a bigger hall, let's start using it for service from next Sunday.

Tony: Thank you God, like I said before, the testimony will take place next Sunday.

The news spread by the warders, that the prisoner commissioner permitted pastor Tony to start using the bigger hall which could contain up to 500 people and for next Sunday the service will now be in the bigger hall. Through out Sunday, Monday and Tuesday Tony was kind of quiet but praying for the fast good news no cancer result in the breast of Lisa the wife of the prison commissioner.

CHAPTER 12

On Sunday the new big hall which takes up to 500 people was full to the capacity including Pastor Toni's mom, and his little brother who is now two years. The church was so full for one big reason but mostly because the church head quarter and their bishop decided to officially ordain Tony on the day without telling Tony to surprise him but he got the feeling as he noticed so many pastors and the bishops presence and heads of the congregation.

Before the church started, John who was in death row but was innocent now a free man, a real born again, strong member of the church, with the post as coordinator, who coordinates the beginning of every service, knew every day plan, had arranged the hall completely different from previous days, with nine seats facing the congregation from the arranged altar, the Bishop seat at the center and one seat placed at the center for Tony to sit.

Everyone sited, as choir singing welcome songs, suddenly Tony walked into the church from the back, ushered to his corner sit, as usual without saying any word, knelt down started praying and crying silently but noticed by everyone, some were so emotionally carried away to the point of crying too. Now the bishop walked to the corner in company of the rest pastors, all raised their hands above Toni's head praying for him, just of sudden a white pigeon flew into the church surprisingly perched on Toni's head and people in the church cried more, singing and dancing out of joy till the pigeon flew away through the door.

Bishop: (Took the microphone) please lower the music (but they don't want to stop the music out of joy and excitement) have any of you seen such miracle before? (Everyone shouted no, Tony was unperturbed by all going around him, still praying) I was ordained pastor 30 years ago, ordained bishop ten years ago, never have I seen such a miracle.

News of this great messenger of God is all over the state, I heard about him but never have I seen such a miracle, I don't know if to call him Tony or Joseph, (every one shouted Jesus but bishop continued, now held Tony up, helped him to his corner seat). As he sat, looked completely different from Tony everyone knew, his face no longer resemble Toni's face but very calm.

Coordinator John: Praise God (everyone responded hallelujah) There is peace in the house of God, can you all imagine where we are now? This supposed to be a prison yard but Apostle or should I call him messenger Tony changed the environment by the extraordinary power given to him by God above.

I was the first person who noticed him not as a regular prisoner as most of us in this prison yard, got the first blessing from him, became more humble and blessed, happy not angry which almost ate me up for wrongly accused for killing a police officer, sentenced to death, on death row, died three times as I was given my last chosen meal before my death but postponed until the officer who killed the officer and arrested me for the killing, turned around and confessed the killing. Praise God, Hallelujah.

Today is a special day, it is not our usual Sunday service. You all know that Tony, special man of God, Graduated last month in the pastoral school, though we have always see him as a pastor but to make it official, the head of the church decided to officially ordain him and give him the full authority as a pastor even though he had been heavenly ordained already. I know some of you never seen his holiness, Bishop Victor Bobe, he is accompanied here for this occasion by these pastors of different church branches, so I now hand you all over to his Holiness Bishop Victor Bobe.

Bishop Victor Bobe: Thank you for your humble introduction, thank you lord for John's saved life. John your story is not new to me, I am now humbly and got the opportunity to meet and touch you. praise God for he is good and always good for ever.

Some times when climbing hills of life, we think he had forgotten us without knowing that with faith the slope hill is just ahead, yourself as a child of God, the worst you can do to yourself is to throw towel in the ring as given up, which is for people with no faith.

Do you remember what Jesus Christ say to his Apostle when they were panicking and shivery thinking they were about drowning in the sea. He called them people of little faith. My people when you believed that you are child of God, nothing, not even when wrongly accused, sentence to death, should make you lose your faith, always have the believe that it is not over until God say so because God might be using you as a good example for others.

So praise God (hallelujah) look at what happened in the church today, the good God, just to fully make today more special than we thought, sent his angel direct from heaven to come and physically anoint Pastor Tony, I called him pastor because God had anointed him already in our presence. What ever we will be doing again, is formality because Pastor Tony is already a pastor as far as we all know.

Pastor Tony, please come to the stage for us to do the formality, who know what is coming next in today's service because I believe more things are happening in today's service, may be you knew already because you are special. We are now to do the ceremony of blessing,ordained you a senior pastor of this church, then I, in the selfish side of me will wait to be the first person to be blessed after your ordination (everyone laugh) or you all don't think I will use this opportunity to ask for my own power blessing from such a special man of God? I don't need to deceive myself, I need all the blessing I can get from him.

Now all the Pastors and the Bishop came around Tony, did the ordination, ordained him as a senior pastor, then Bishop knelt in front of Pastor Tony who blessed him, then each pastor knelt down for pastor Toni's blessing. Now Pastor Tony asked for a bucket of water which John brought. As pastor Tony cried to his heavenly father for the blessing of the water, tree other birds flew into the church and out(everyone was surprise) Tony now sprayed everyone in the church with the blessing water, as he finished, called out John and in presence of everyone, ordained him as a deacon of the church.

Pastor Tony: Thank you all, thank you all but most of all, everyone here should thank the prison commissioner for giving us this space for the service and I know by next year we will ask him for space of land where to build the bigger church. God almighty will give us the money to build a church here in the prison yard, a church that could contain 20,000 people, I know it's on the way, so thank you commissioner of prison.

I am having the feeling as I am talking, that someone want to tell us something special today, so if anyone in this church want to give us good news, the floor is open.

(Before he finished making the announcement, about 10 people including the prison commissioner and his family who came out straight to pastor Tony, took the microphone).

The wife of the commissioner: Praise God, (People responded hallelujah), but she said "I did not hear you all very well" I say praise God (now very loud, everyone shouted hallelujah as she knelt down crying as Pastor Tony held her hand and got her up).

You all should listen very well because none of you know how blessed we are to get such a man of God in platter of gold and I pray God will not take him out of this place even after the so called serving sentence. Last Sunday my husband and I brought the bad news of me been diagnosed of breast cancer and to see the group of doctors on Tuesday for plans on what to do, but the man of God pastor Tony asked me to kneel down, prayed and said "you don't have cancer", go on Tuesday and found out that the diagnose will be reversed as you not having cancer.

We went to the hospital to see seven doctors cancer expert, first of all, I was hooked up to a big machine for one hour, checking every part of my body only to turned off machine and say to me congratulation we can not see any cancer cell active in your breast and in rest of your body, then my husband said to them "I don't understand what you are saying" but the doctors pulled out this two medical reports saying (she read it to everyone hearing) After all the machine medical checkup for cancer cells in Lisa's both breast and the rest of her body, the result came cancer negative. (At this point both the prison commissioner and the wife started crying praising Pastor Tony and God).

One of the people who came out for testimony said "ask my mom, mom stop crying but get up", she brought me to this church service, I came here this morning blind, as I had been blind for the past one year, but as the anointed water torched my head, I don't know what happened, the blind darkness just disappeared, now I can see everyone in this church, praise God and God bless pastor Tony.

Now the prison commissioner took the microphone and announced that the land at the northwest is given to the church for whatever you want to build any time. (Everyone just shouting and praising God and Pastor Tony.

Pastor Tony: By next Sunday service, if you know anyone with one problem or the other, as you are coming for service, come with them and on that service our preaching and teaching will be relationship and love. Everyone should get up for the final blessing of the day.

Father how great you are, we worship and bless you, father we thank and bless you for all you have being doing in our life but we still ask for more, father guide and protect everyone in this service to get to their respective homes in peace but not pieces (everyone say amen).

Everyone went to the hall for light refreshment then everyone left for the day.

CHAPTER 13

Before the next Sunday, the news of Pastor Tony was everywhere, all waiting for Sunday to attend the service, some with one sickness or the other. As the mother of Brenda now suffering from cancer, Brenda and her husband, Michael with the two moms, Brenda's mom and Michael's mom suffering from partial blindness, all came for the service.

The church was so filled up as some people got to the church as early as 6am, some came from far away cities for the service. All Michael/ Brenda knew was the news of this great miracles man of God in the church in the prison yard but they never know the man of God everyone is talking about is Tony.

As the service was to start, the choir singing, Tony as usual practice before starting any service, was on his knees praying but faced the back of the church, everyone just point finger at him, talking about how good he is, just a sudden Tony got up, faced the congregation as everyone applauded, getting up from their seats shouting hallelujah, the music very loud for up to 10 minutes as he walked slowly towards the pulpit (as he pray after each step) but as he was almost at the pulpit, Michael/Brenda kind of recognized the pastor to be Tony, were frozen, could not alter a word but looking at each other, at last Brenda say to Michael,

Brenda: Michael is this not Tony you falsely testified against in court?

Michael: Thank for all your manipulation, don't use such word, you plotted it, made me to carry it out even though he never did any crime from day one (the stealing of the Gucci bag). I was stupid falling into your temptation.

59

(As pastor Tony blessed the water in the bucket, walked around the big church, sprayed the water by dipping the branches of palm frond in the bucket and spraying it to the congregation praying and walking around the congregation. Now he got to the area of Brenda, Michael, Michael's mom and Brenda's mom, sprayed and past.

Brenda: Michael, he recognized us, he looked at you as he past, mom, do you know who the man of God is?

Bay: (Brenda's mom) No, how will I know?

Brenda: Mom, don't you remember Tony, the one Michael testified against in the court?

Bay: Don't say so, your bro (she past out before saying brother).

There was commotion and confusion in the church. John went to pastor Tony and informed him. That a lady past out over there.

Tony: You all should go carry her to the alter. (Which they did as Tony knelt down praying calling on God to hear his cry and prove how good God is). As they brought her to the alter in front of Tony as she was lifeless while all the congregation frozen.

Tony: (Looked up, started praying) Thank you God, thank you God, I worship you, give you your glory because you deserve it. Here is your servant (asked for her name)

Brenda: Bay, Tony she is my mother, she is my mother, please help, I am so sorry for all I did to you.

Tony: My God, your servant Bay fell asleep, I know she is not dead but asleep, oh God my father show me your power, you have life and death, give bay life not death, to extend you good work (Tony told them to bring the bucket with the holy water, use his palm to take a lot of water, rubbed it on Bay's face). Bay wake up, you are not dead but asleep, (Bay woke up crying and praising God) got up. John please get her a chair, she is going to be by the alter with me throughout the service, everyone should go back to their seats. But Brenda and Michael could not go back to their seat, only standing in front of Tony stiffed.

John: Please can two of you move to your chairs?

Michael: Please we want to talk to the congregation first.

John: (Went to pastor Tony) Pastor, the couple refused to go to their chairs until they are allowed to speak to the congregation.

Pastor Tony: Okay, give them the microphone.

Michael: (Started crying) good afternoon everyone, I don't know how to start, but before I start, I want to use this opportunity to say to you pastor Tony, as man of God, forgive me for sending you to where you are now, please forgive me, I don't know what came into me to accept the manipulation, I am very sorry.

Brenda: (Crying took the microphone, looked at the pastor Tony and it go like this) Pastor Tony, your friend Michael lied against you sending you to prison as he wrongly testified against you in the court but I did the worst for first of all getting you arrested, sent to police custody wrongly accusing you for stealing my Gucci bag which was not stolen in the first place, also wrongly accused you of killing Vicent and made poor Michael wrongly testified against you which made the Judge condemned you and sentenced you to 20 years for a crime you never committed. Please Tony can you ever forgive us for all these done to you? You even lost your dad because of all these, please forgive me pastor Tony.

(Now Brenda's mom begged as she sat to have the microphone which was given to her.)

Bay: Please can the man of God come by my right side and Brenda to my left side because I want to share a secret to both of you which only me in the whole world knew. (They both did as she requested while Brenda crying) Man of God Tony, I found out that you and your sister Brenda were one week apart, you and Brenda are brother and sister all children of Dr. Anthony, I found out at Dr. Anthony's funeral and kept it inside me till now.

Brenda stumbled trying to fall but pastor Tony held her, got her up as everyone in the church were in shock while some crying including pastor Toni's mom who walked to pastor Tony and Brenda saying to Brenda, here is your other brother, Emma as we now know you as Dr. Anthony's child, this one came as I slept with Dr. Anthony the only night he shared together with Tony.

The congregation frozen but watching, Tony took the hand of the little brother, holding him now, held Brenda's hand and say to her, can you hold Emma's other hand for us to make circle, which she did.

Tony: (Looking up) cried out loud, Oh God, what can I say but to thank you for this day, weeks, months and years past and years to come, oh my heavenly father, you are beyond human comprehension. This is why it was said "no one knows tomorrow" never say never.

All these years Brenda and I did not know we are siblings. Thank God, blessed today, this is a wonderful day, a day never to be forgotten in history of mankind for making this possible, praise God almighty. (They hugged one another, now told everyone to go to their chairs which they did). My congregation, is our God not great? (Everyone answered) yes he is. Do we still have time to talk about today's main topic?

Everyone: Yes, man of God we do.

Pastor Tony: What is the days main topic?

Everyone: Love and relationship.

Pastor: What is different between love and relationship? Which of them come first, between love and relationship? Who know the answer?

Some one got up: My name is Carthrine. To me, love come first before relationship.

Someone got up: My name is Debora. I will like to know the kind of relationship we are talking about because there are many types of love e.g the love of parents, the love of someone you intend to make love with, so pastor, which of the love are we talking about? If it is the love of parents and the relationship of child and parent, the unconditional love come first before the relationship started, parents started loving the child before the child was born, if it is sibling, love come first before relationship and if it is the love that you intend to one day make love with the person, courtship come first, relationship, then love come to nurtured the relationship.

Pastor Tony: Praise God, (all answered hallelujah) love and relation is a very big topic which is going to take a lot of our time to discuss today. Starting with the question, what is love?

Wikipedia put it this way, Love is considered to be positive and negative, with its virtue representing human kindness, compassion and affection as "the unselfish loyal and benevolent concern for the good of others. Some say that love is the most spectacular, indescribable, deep euphoric feeling for someone.

Now that we all know the definition of love but not elaborated based on the fact that there are many types of love, for example, parental love which most of time is unconditional, parent will be ready to give up their life but to protect their children. There was a saying "baby monkey is very ugly but the mom still love him" even chicken, do you all know mother chicken to be vicious? Go and try to pick up any of her chicks. At the same time there are some percent of men who planting children here and there, when their baby mother call them for one thing or the other for their children, one way or the other, the bad men will give one excuse or another (you are not a parent, you only donated eggs) but when they discovered the child making any achievement, they will want to be noticed first even before the baby nine month carrier. Why do you want to reap what you did not sow? What of love of sibling, they may be fighting at home but the moment someone try to hurt their sibling, then the love of sibling will show up, you will not know when you started protecting your sibling.

The love we are talking today is the love which may end you too become husband and wife, build up one family, may even get the blessing of bring another human into this world, good or bad, thief, athletic, pastor, Judge, even prostitute. All the above mentioned are contributors of all our daily living, or don't you think a beggar on the street also contributes to our every day living? Or do you all think only the rich people, doctors, police, pilots, pastors, Reverend fathers and Reverend sisters are the only contributors?

My brothers and sisters, life is a circle, if any part no matter how small is removed from the circle, it will no more be a circle because it will not complete to make it a circle, I hope you all understand where I'm coming from when it come to human circle, as we all know, the particular love I am talking about, love come first before relationship and true love is the glue that keeps the relationship strong and solid.

Lovemaking now is deep and holy, a true journey but not rape, you are committing crime not getting to the love summit. When you really love someone in this category, you most truly love the person like said in the 10 commandments, look at it this way, if you love someone, will you no matter what took place, like to punch the person, man or woman? Will you tell lies on the person? Steal what belong to the person? Try to deceive and manipulate the person? Cheat on the person? Even kill the person physically, psychologically or emotionally?

If you truly love someone, you will not only be thinking on what to gain from the person, always thinking on what to do to make my love one happy, but I don't mean you have to be a fool because you are in love for example, when your lover say go and kill or go and steal, you do so because pastor Tony told us about love, the same pastor is now saying that you should not become a fool as you are in love.

Now come to relationship, the most important way to build a good and lasting building, start from good foundation. when building foundation is not solid, it may even fall before the roofing. To build a good and lasting relationship, do we first try to know much about the person? The dos and don'ts of the person? Let's put it these ways.

Do we first try to know their dos and don'ts?

Do we try to know their favorite things, even goal in life?

Do we try to know their blood type?

Do we like to know how they like making love? Mostly men, do any of you trying to find out what brings the woman to the top of her mountain? Or you think every woman don't know what brings them to the top of their mountain. Most of the time men so focused on their selfish and trying to get to the top of their mountain because as you allow them to your down town, as long as they are active, they will get to the top of their mountain with the woman or without her even getting midway to the top of her mountain.

Okay, when you get to the top of you mountain, do you thank or found out if the woman got to the top of her mountain yet. You the woman, let's say you don't get to the top of your mountain, do you ever pick the courage to explain to him how you want him to do it in order for you to get to the top of your mountain. Now that you get to the top of your mountain, do you show appreciation to each other for this love journey?

Women, thinking you are doing men favor for accepting making love with men when it come to climbing to the top of their mountain, you are doing favor to you too, try make the best out of it. You all know some women could be with men, have children together but never get to the top of the mountain.

How many of you at the beginning of every year, give your other one plain sheet of paper to put down things he/she did last year that you do not like also tell your other one what he/she did that you appreciated and want to discuss how to fix things each other wrongly did to one another last year.

You can use the opportunity to tell him that you never enjoyed the love making last year and tell him how you want it down. It is good you tell him, he might think he was doing the right thing not knowing he was scoring poorly but when this is known and fixed, I promise you, your relationship will get stronger, on the other hand, if you don't let on another know what was going wrong, it will never be fixed and it may lead to the end of the relationship.

Please don't feel shy about it, if you don't enjoy any food given to you, 90 percent you will express your dissatisfaction, so why must you feel shy to express the ways you get to satisfaction.

I am about closing the topic of the day which is very big topic but I want to ask you all these few relationship questions and let's answer them.

1. How many percent of keeping marriage do women have? Answer is 80 to 85% to be successful.

2. Who cherish wedding ring more, between man and woman? Answer -woman; appreciate wedding rings more than men.

3. When a woman stop wearing her wedding ring, what does she mean? Answer is that she is no more interested in the marriage.

I want you all go home and put a thought on the above mentioned. You will get satisfy or enjoy that kind of food of mine?

My brothers and sisters we have to stop now, the day is getting late,some are very hungry, hopping to see next week to discuss more about facts of life.

My sister Brenda and Emma, both of you should come to the alter, Brenda go and bring Emma from my mom and come to the alter (which she did, prayed and blessed them). Thank you my God, today is a special day in the life of your servant, my Good Heavenly father I am grateful. Sister Brenda and Emma, go back to you seats.

Pastor Tony: Brothers and sisters, you all should help me thank God for making us see a day like this, thank you my God, bless brother Michael, sister Brenda, the police officers that arrested me, the prosecutor and the judge who sentenced me and personally ordered the authority to send me to this facility, oh my God I can not do anything without your help, my God, from the bottom of my heart all is new, for they are forgiven. I only thank you my heavenly father because from day one, you and only you knew the plans, thank you my heavenly father for making all these possible. If all these did not happen, May be I could have not be where we all are now, all glory to your name. I pray for the soul of my biological father and soul of Vicent. I pray for the family members left behind, pray for each and every one of us here to get to our respective homes in peace. Amen.

See you all next Sunday.

CHAPTER 14

As the serviced ended Michael decided to rush home as Brenda begged pastor Toni's mom to stay behind with her little brother, went to pastor Tony to informed him that she is going to buy some dinner for all of the family, herself and the two moms to have their first together dinner (all accepted and she left). Came back after 30minutes with different kinds of food which all of them had as family. It was like day and night, ways everyone behaved from that moment, the kind of love Brenda now showing to pastor Tony and Emma, phone numbers and addresses exchanged and everyone left to their respective places. On Monday Esso (Pastor Toni's case manager) after observing what took place at the service as she attended the Sunday service, now went to the city hall, talked to the district attorney to reopen the case as the case was a set up right from the beginning to the end.

The D.A accepted her request after her information on all that took place at the service on Sunday. The D.A met the same judge, judge Vera Elu who presided the case, gave her reason to reopen the case. The judge agreed and after all said and down the date for now court hearing was set also issued subpoena for Brenda and Michael to appear in the court on the very day (Sept.10.2004). The mother of pastor Tony and lawyer Cohen were notified and on (Sept.10.2004) everyone came to the court, the court was so full to the point of many people standing outside the court.

Court Clark: All stand as the judge is Walking into the court room, all sit now as the judge sat.

Prosecutor: Good morning your worship; good morning everyone, four years ago we thought this case was over, never will I believe that we all will convene as we are now for this same case, your worship on 10th of June 1999, Tony Hugo was found guilty of the murder of Vicent _Mark _ _ _ based on the evidence before you, sentenced to 20 years imprisonment, case closed but your worship, it was like magic or good luck that Tony Hugo's story turned for good. It did not stop there, the collaborators eventually confessed that all the story right from the beginning to the end were all made up, wrongly accused innocent Tony of the crime which lead him to the prison. I was even in the church when the confessions were made at the present of everyone. Your worship, after going through my thought and report, I will like to reopen the case before you. Thank you your worship.

Judge Vera Elu: Wonder shall never end. Prosecutor as I can tell, Tony is sitting over there but are the collaborators any where to be found?

Prosecutor: Yes your worship, they are in the court room, even the police officers involved at the beginning of the case and the officers at the second case are in the court room too.

Judge Vera Elu: Can you call all of them out?

Prosecutor: Everyone involved in the case of Tony Hugo stealing of Brenda's Gucci bag, should come out, you all should be sited in front right side of the judge, then introduce yourself to the court for documentation.

Brenda: Your worship (as she started crying) My name is Brenda Bee who wrongly accused my brother pastor Tony of stealing my Gucci bag, which lead to his first arrest. Brother Tony, it was a lie, you never stole my Gucci bag, please like I said to you in the church "Please find a space in your heart to forgive me. (Tony gave her sign of peace). The prosecutor did not allow her to start the second case yet.

Police officer Nud and officer Sonny: Your worship both of us where the first officers who arrested Tony from school, took him to the custody, made him to urinate in a cup, beat him up, made him to drink his urine, called him all kinds of racial names, all these happened during the interrogation, he did all we forced him to do yet saying he did not steal Brenda's Gucci bag. Please Pastor Tony as man of God, please forgive us for all the bad things we did to you. (Tony gave sign of peace).

Prosecutor: Please you all should go to your seats, now to the second case. All involved should come up, do as we just witnessed. (They came out, this time Brenda, Michael, the officers that went to arrest Tony then killed Dr. Anthony).

Brenda: Your worship here we go again, I am the architect of the beginning and the end of all these cases, I am the monster who engineered all these, I don't know what came into me, I made Michael to be involved of wrongly testifying against his best friend Tony, please Tony my brother, my life is in your hands, forgive me and Michael, my husband Michael, please forgive me for wrongly getting you involved and got your palms stained with murder blood.

Judge Vera Elu: Brenda, Where are the Gucci bag now?

Brenda: The Gucci bag and Michael's cell phone were thrown into the river Brimley.

Judge Vera Elu: Why?

Brenda: Your worship, to cover the evidence of no one seeing the bag and to stop the checking of the cell phone to find out if Tony really called Michael, saying he will be killing Vicent which never took place. Brother Tony, Michael and everyone in this court,(crying) I Brenda Bee......, from the bottom of my heart ask for your forgiveness.

Michael: ...... Pastor Tony, I don't know what to call you, please I am Michael Mole....., I was only a big fool, to betray our friendship since grade five, pastor Tony, please take it as work of devil, you know how long we had been. I fell into temptation and will never happen in my life again, I promise you all, it will never happen again. (Tony show peace sign to him).

The three police officers: we are sorry to you pastor Tony, please forgive us for what took place, we took your father from you(Tony crying but still showed peace sign).

Judge Vera Elu: Everyone should go back to their seats while I take 30minutes break, at the break, I want to speak to the prosecutor.

Court Clerk: Arise after 30 minutes.

The judge came back with the prosecutor after making some outside calls for advice on how to bring this problem to an end.

Judge Vera Elu: (After settling down on her chair), I spoke to different past, I will take their advices, but nothing will replace what pastor Tony went through in life due to gang up, racism but we will make the best out of what we learnt in this case but like I mentioned above, there is nothing we will do to balance what pastor Tony went through for crimes never committed. I have to first, on behave of this city say to you. Tony, we are sorry for what you went through, there will be some financial reward for what you went through, at least $10,000,000 will be paid to you, you will be released from prison immediately and by next week (Sept 19ᵗʰ 2004) I will like Brenda and Michael to appear in this court, before then, I must have come to conclusion on their punishment for it had been said the wicked shall not go unpunished, they brought problems to the city and I will use this two people as scapegoat so that in near future people will think before acting in such a wicked acts. It will be unfair if we all go to our respective homes with out Pastor Tony not speaking in today's court sitting. So can you come to speak to the court on all you gathered today.

Pastor Tony: Your worship please can I pray silently for five minutes? If permitted.

Judge Vera Elu: You are permitted.

Pastor Tony: Thank you your worship. (Then knelt down in a corner, prayed for God to guide him on things to say). Your worship, people from this great city, thank you all for all you went through for the past four years but I can not thank God my heavenly father enough for the blessing and opportunity given to me in this issue, how likely am I to be the one chosen to be the message of peace and love. Your worship, please, Michael and my sister Brenda had gone through a lot, self reflection, personally, I had forgiven them from the bottom of my heart, prayed for both of them to take it easy with themselves because if there was no crime, there will be no pardon mostly when there is reflection and asked for forgiveness. It is always good to forgive but it is more better when the person that offended you asked for forgiveness because it will be valued by the person forgiven after asking for the forgiveness. Praise God almighty for chosen me to carry out this message and mission of teaching the power of please, thanks, sorry and forgiveness. I praise you my God, I worship you my God, to you all the praises will ever go to, I am only a tool to be used by you. Your worship I heard all your comments. Please let me deal with each comment and instruction as stated above.

1. I will plead on behave of Michael and my sister Brenda. Please be merciful and forgive them as both realized their wrong actions.

2. Please as you instructed my immediate release from prison, I would like to go back to the prison for one week, at least to stay there till the coming Sunday to get myself prepared for outside world also to do my final preaching over there as a prisoner.

3. Finally, as you ordered the city to pay me $10,000,000, $5,000,000 out of the $10,000,000 will be used to build the new church in the prison yard where I will be coming to celebrated the Sunday service from outside prison also, will have canceling office in the new church. Thank you your worship.

Judge Vera Elu: I will look into your first request, your second request is accepted so you will be taken back to the prison and for your number 3 request, your mind is set as a good person. Court is close till next Sept 26th 2004.

Court Clerk: Arise (everyone standing as the judge walked out of her bench out of the court room.) As everyone left the court, all talking about all that took place in the court room, praising pastor Tony for all he did in the court room but most of all, the decision to use half of the money awarded to him for what he went through in these cases to build church in the prison yard surprised everyone. As Brenda and Michael got home with no word from Michael, even when Brenda was thanking God for brother (Pastor Tony), Michael did not say any word. After the dinner, Michael went to the room and lay down, Brenda finally went to bed after talking with the big new discovered big brother (pastor Tony) only to wake up at night looking for her husband Michael but found his lifeless hanged body with a note which he wrote.

Dear pastor Tony, my wife Brenda, my mom and all members of this city, I am sorry to put you all through this. I am too ashamed for all I did, even though pastor Tony my child hood friend as man of God had forgiven me for testifying against him, I found it very difficult to forgive myself and don't know where to start but just to end it. Bye Bye.

Brenda called the police, notified her brother pastor Tony, Michael mother and her own mom. After all said and done on Saturday, Michael was criminated and ash thrown to the river as always his ending choice.

CHAPTER 15

The news of all that took place in the court, pastor Toni's plan of using half of the awarded money for the wrongly accused and punished to him, planning to use $5,000,000 which is half of the $10,000,000 to build a big church in the prison yard also the hanging of Michael (all these news were all over the city).

On Sunday the church got so full, more than ever as everyone want to attend Pastor Toni's last church service as a prisoner. Now that the church service started as usual with the singing and dancing waiting for the pastor to show up, but to everyone's surprise, Pastor Tony walking into the church on his prison uniform, went to his usual corner, knelt down for prayer. (Pastor Tony walk to the pulpit as everyone clapping but surprised with his dressing as a prisoner).

Pastor Tony: Good morning my brothers and sisters, before we start today's service, we should pray for the soul of our brother Michael who passed last week, I pray that God will have mercy, forgive him any sin he had sinned knowingly or unknowingly, may his soul rest in peace, also I pray that God will guide and protect my sister Brenda the wife of Michael, the mother of Michael, all love ones left behind also the entire city. I pray that you God will not allow such a sad story to take place in our city again, Amen.

Today is the last day I will be doing church service with you all as a prisoner, which will teach you my brothers and sisters that no condition is permanent in this world. I will be leaving this prison yard to my mother's house as I finished today's church service (at this time a lot of people mostly prisoners started crying very loud) why are you crying? I am not going to stop coming here for church service with you all and I want to let you all know that I had been hired by the prison commissioner to be the general overseer of canceling department of this prison. (Now everyone started clapping and jumping up for joy) my brothers and sisters, one big teaching I am brining to each and every one of you today is to know and have power of these four.

1. Power of asking for forgiveness when you offended anyone.

2. Power of please, knowing how to say please

3. Power of thanks, to know how to be appreciative and use the word thank you

4. The last but not the least, when begged for forgiveness, no matter the anger when the offender beg you for forgiveness, think of gift and power of forgiveness and forgive the offender. If not for anything, it will make you lighter because when you refused the offer, it will be self victimization because of the heavy heart you created for yourself.

The way things will be taking place now in our Sunday service, I will like other outsiders from this prison yard to know that I will be coming every Sunday for service though for my brothers here, you will be given my schedule of being in the office. God is very wonderful, he do his things in his ways.

If all these things that happened to me did not happen, do you all believe that this mission could have been created? But because he had his plans and created how the plans should take place. This is why when things or plans are not working the ways planed, don't just give up, see it that you are climbing the hill of life only pray that things will come in your favor at end, let's say Amen (everyone say Amen).

When the confrontation was taking place from Brenda for 12 years, to the point of me been sent to the prison due to what started from her, who will ever tell Brenda and I that we are brother and sister, may be if we had known that we are brother and sister; she could have not accused me in the first place, may be I could have not been here as I am now but for his plans to materialize, that was why everything took place these ways.

My brothers and sisters I am going to bless the water in the bucket spraying it to everyone as I walk around the church (Which he did, as he was spraying the holy water on people, so many miracles took place, people crying and giving all kinds of testimony but at end he blessed everyone and as usual went to his corner to pray for everyone's home going safely as people departed.

Pastor Tony after the service had a very elaborated dinner with the rest inmates, prayed for each and every one of them, made them to believe in themselves, always trust in God because with God all is possible if they believe in him. After the dinner, Pastor Tony packed his belongings and with the vehicles of Brenda's mom, his mom's and the vehicle of the dad's wife who eventually joined them, they all drove to his mom's house where a lot of plans were made.

CHAPTER 16

The very big church in the prison yard was eventually built with the $5,000,000 donated by Pastor Tony, became the pastor of the church at the prison yard at the same time working as the main consoler of the prison where peace is noticed by everyone, to the point that prisoners of other facilities pray to be taken to this facility. All came to pass, Pastor Tony with the money at hand developed the piece of land shown to him by the step mother saying that the land belong to Dr. Anthony.

As the piece of the land happen to be big, Pastor Tony since he do not want any of them, the step mom, Brenda and her mom, his mom, the little brother Emmer and himself to ever be separated, in so doing, he built four big identical houses in the same compound, one for the step mother, one for his sister Brenda and her mom, one for his mom and the little brother Emmer and one for himself and from then, all of them lived together in happiness like people in town never seen. As he continue with his God mission now making people to believe that what will be will be no matter how long it takes, will be as long as you have faith.

No one plan where to be born, who the parent will be. If there is any telescope for us to view how the world coming as a child, is going to be, the population couldn't have been so many. You might end up a president, very rich or great person but as you view it and see how your world journey is going to be from the day born till the day you die, after viewing the life journey, many will decide to stay in the spiritual world than coming to go through the ups and downs ahead.

They are so many ups and downs in the world we live. Some people fell with no courage to stand up, forgotten that the down fall of a person is not the end of the person's life though some gives up easily while some never give up, with the hope that tomorrow is pregnant, no one knows what tomorrow will bring or have for you, like young Tony Hugo who went through roughness of life from conception till half of his life time, falling from frying pan to fire, many a time except from tiger to be picked up by lion but never give up hope knowing that we live and die by faith.

Learning so many lessons from mother nature who happen to be a great teacher, teaching us all never to be dwelling so much on our past fallings, to be able to see the future. Always believe that what happened to you could take you to unexpected good place, young Tony Hugo was good example.

Again the great teacher never stop teaching us so many lessons,here is the latest lesson by mother Nature, the lesson of corona virus by mama Nature who taught us a lot about life, in this case, she made us to know that the world we all thought to be very big happen to be so small but very deep in the sense that the air which touched Lin in China last week could get to Linda in Canada today,may get to lokilo in U.S.A next week and get to lui in Chad by two weeks from now.

You know most of us forget that the two most important connecting things mother Nature have for us all,her children, be you in China, Canada, Benin Republic or anywhere in the world,are water and air but one is faster (Air) She continue reminding us all that every new day brings us one day close to the most perfect treasure mother Nature have for each and every one of us.

She made it so equal for her children, us all no matter your richness,your poverty,be you sleeping on the street, sleeping in the pent house, beautiful or ugly, tall or short, black or white, Asian or African, American or from Ubulu Ezemu,sinner or good person. She shared it equally with no partiality, so kept secret to make it more exciting, made people scared to get their share but do you have choice not getting your share? No, death is inevitable no one escapes death. So do the best out of every day you live in this world because today may be the day Mother nature have for you to take your share.

CPSIA information can be obtained
at www.ICGtesting.com
Printed in the USA
BVHW081712150920
588720BV00001B/42